SAVED BY THE MILLIONAIRE NEXT DOOR 2

KRYSTAL ARMSTEAD

Saved By The Millionaire Next Door 2

Copyright © 2024 by Krystal Armstead

All rights reserved.

Published in the United States of America.

All rights reserved. No part of this publication may be reproduced, distributed, or transmitted in any form or by any means, including photocopying, recording, or other electronic or mechanical methods, without the prior written permission of the publisher, except in the case of brief quotations embodied in critical reviews and certain other noncommercial uses permitted by copyright law. For permission requests, please contact: www.colehartsignature.com

This is a work of fiction. Names, characters, places, and incidents either are the products of the author's imagination or are used fictitiously. Any resemblance of actual persons, living or dead, businesses, companies, events, or locales is entirely coincidental. The publisher does not have any control and does not assume any responsibility for author or third-party websites or their content.

The unauthorized reproduction or distribution of this copyrighted work is a crime punishable by law. No part of the book may be scanned, uploaded to or downloaded from file sharing sites, or distributed in any other way via the Internet or any other means, electronic, or print, without the publisher's permission. Criminal copyright infringement, including infringement without monetary gain, is investigated by the FBI and is punishable by up to five years in federal prison and a fine of $250,000 (www.fbi.gov/ipr/).

This book is licensed for your personal enjoyment only. Thank you for respecting the author's work.

Published by Cole Hart Signature, LLC.

Mailing List

To stay up to date on new releases, plus get information on contests, sneak peeks, and more,

Go To The Website Below...

www.colehartsignature.com

CHAPTER ONE
GIA

"Crazy bitch, did you take your meds today? Gabby laughed, waking me out of my sleep.

"Shut up, Gabby." I rolled over in my cot. Well, *tried* to roll over. I was cuffed to the railing of my bed in the psych ward of the University of Maryland Medical Center, awaiting my fuckin' court date.

Those niggas set you up, Gabby growled. *Your sister ratted you out.*

"It wasn't Brielle's husband who I was fuckin'. Marley did this." I put my hands over my ears, trying to stop myself from hearing Gabby's demonic voice.

Brielle's boyfriend is a well-known lawyer. He researches cases for a living. He was probably researching you this entire time, Gabby conversed with me.

I turned on my back. "Do you think Marley was talking to Brielle's boyfriend?"

More like fuckin' Brielle's boyfriend. Gabby laughed out loud. *We overheard those nurse bitches talking about the way they saw Rigel dancin' with Marley at the skating rink. Hand around her* neck and shit. *Pussy makes a nigga bold. He's fuckin' the lining out that pussy.*

"Do you think she fucked my sister's boyfriend to get back at me for fuckin' Knight? Is this shit *my* fault?" I sat up in bed.

She did tell you to stay away from him, dummy, Gabby snapped. *Can't never keep your fuckin' legs closed. Give that thang a rest, shit. That nigga is married, and so are you.*

"And where is my nigga since I'm married, Gabby?" I huffed, lying back down in bed.

"Right here." Trap's voice snapped me out of my conversation with one of the pieces of me.

I looked to my left, eyeing Trap sitting in the recliner in the far corner of my room. I was so out of it that I didn't even see my handsome husband sitting in the chair. He stood, dressed in a fresh white t-shirt, dark jeans, and white and gray Jordans. Gold chains were draped around his neck. His long hair was braided back. I knew the bitch who was one of his dancers braided his hair. The way she always looked back at him on stage when he was performing let me know something was going on between the two.

"How long have you been sitting there?" I asked as he approached my side, pulling up a stool.

Trap plopped on the stool. "Since this morning when your lawyer called me."

"He called about my court date?" I hesitated to ask.

Trap shook his head, his dark eyebrows lowering into a frown. "Nah, he called about your *sister's* court date."

I turned to him, confused. "My sister? Brielle's here?"

Trap wasn't sure how to put his thoughts into words. I could tell by the way he rested his forearms on his thighs, fingers intertwined, that he had some news he wasn't sure I could handle. "Nah, Londyn, your twin sister."

I was still lost. I shook my head, not comprehending what he was saying to me. "I don't have a twin sister."

Trap disagreed. "She was admitted here when she was eighteen. She's been here for nine years. She helped you escape that night. She was the one who killed those guards and injured those nurses. She confessed a few days ago. The nurses finally admitted that you sat in a corner, rocking, while Londyn attacked them. After she killed the guards, she came and got you out of the corner."

Flashes of that night bolted through my mind. I remember looking up into a face that mirrored mine as she pulled me off the floor. Her hands were covered in blood. I thought I was having an out-of-body experience.

"Why-why am I cuffed to this bed if I didn't hurt those people?" I asked, feeling tears slide over the bridge of my nose.

Trap nodded toward my hand. "You punched one of the CNAs when she told you 'welcome back.'"

I looked down at my cuffed hand, eying my bruised knuckles.

"You didn't tell me you have a baby girl, babygirl." Trap looked into my face.

I looked at him. "Where is my baby? You already took my son from me! Did you take my daughter from me, too? Give her back!" I sat up in bed, reaching for him, trying to grab him by the collar.

"Who is her father?" Trap's nostrils flared. When I didn't respond, he already knew the answer. "He's been here?"

"Every night for a fuckin' year, Trap," I snapped.

"I didn't know," Trap whispered, scratching his head. "What do you want me to do?"

I laughed out loud. "You're asking me that shit now? After he raped me under this hospital's supervision? If I'm not in trouble, get me out of here! If I didn't kill those officers or hurt those nurses, get me out of here!"

"The state won't drop the charges until the hearing. Until your sister confesses in court and the nurses testify on your behalf, you can't leave. Your court date is next Monday. I tried to come see you, Gia." Trap's brown eyes searched my face. "I kept you out of the media for the past few months, for your protection, for–"

"For *your* protection." I scoffed. "You didn't want your fans to know you're married to a crazy bitch. Where is my son? I haven't seen him in a year! I wasn't trying to hurt him!"

"Well, you would have if I didn't get there when I did," Trap reminded me.

"I was broken," I whimpered.

"You still are. I was trying to fix you when I sent you here." Trap tried to reach for my hand. When I flinched, he exhaled deeply and sat up on the stool.

"Yeah? Well, look how that turned out!" I cried and laughed at the same time. "My father has gotten away with so much for so long, and no one has put an end to it. Who's going to stop him? Why hasn't anyone stopped him?"

Trap didn't know what to say except, "You could've told me that you were in trouble instead of telling the staff that you didn't want any visitors."

I shot him an angry look over my shoulder. "Matthew got in despite the fact that I didn't want fuckin' visitors, Trap. I don't want to hear it. When they let me out of here, I never want to see you again. Go on with your life, which I'm sure you already have." He didn't think I noticed he wasn't wearing his wedding band. "When that lawyer comes back, have him file the divorce papers. I want out of this. You could've made a way, but you didn't, and I'm done."

"I loved you with everything I had, Geor'Gia." Trap called

me by my government name, which no one ever did except him.

"Yeah, 'loved' as in past tense." I smacked my lips.

"Nephy is with my mom, and so is Rhion. She's beautiful, just like her mother." Trap stood from the stool.

I fought back the tears.

"We're married, so as far as the courts are concerned, she's mine despite the fact that the DNA will prove otherwise. He can't take her from you." Trap gripped my shoulder as I broke down in tears. "You're a lot to handle, babe. Every time I tried to put your pieces back together, I ended up cutting myself. I put you in that place to protect you. You have to know that."

I nodded, drying my tears with my free hand as I turned to him. "You better not have that bitch around my kids, Trap. I'm coming for them when I get out."

"It's in your best interest to stay, even after your court date tomorrow," Dr. Jaliyah Marcus told me the following day in her office. "Once the court determines that you didn't help Londyn murder the security guards or injure those nurses, you'll be free to go, though I don't recommend you leave. You need help, Gia." She watched the tears slide down my cheeks.

"I thought—" I choked back tears. "I thought I was having an out-of-body experience the night I left here. I don't even remember the majority of that night, but I do remember seeing my face. What I *thought* was my face, which was actually hers. She's prettier than me. I should've known she wasn't me."

"You two look exactly alike." Dr. Marcus laughed a little, removing her reading glasses from her face. "Well, she is a favorite around here. She's been here since she was eighteen. Her foster family owns this facility, ya know. The Camerons.

They married her off to another rich family of Southern politicians when she was just seventeen. You heard of the LePonts? She married Kennedy LePont, the senator in Raleigh."

I looked at the doctor. That cracker worked with my father. My father was running for senator and was probably going to win based on the fact that his best friend was already in office and would probably serve another six-year term when he was re-elected.

"How did my sister end up here?" I hesitated to ask.

"She says she killed her, and I quote, 'cracker-ass-bitch' mother-in-law because she kept calling Londyn a 'black nigger bitch.' Said her mother-in-law made her eat with a separate fork, spoon, knife, plate, and cup. She said her mother-in-law made her come in the back entrance and even had the maids going behind her, sanitizing everything she touched.

"Londyn said that one day, she saw her mother-in-law on her balcony smoking a cigar. She snuck up behind her with a sheet that her mother-in-law made the staff wash because she'd heard that Londyn had touched it. Londyn managed to tie the sheet to the leg of the umbrella table before sneaking up behind the old woman. She wrapped the sheet around the woman's neck, then pushed her over the edge. Londyn said she smiled when she heard her mother-in-law's neck crack." The doctor laughed a little with tears in her eyes.

I looked at her, confused as to why she was violating her patient's confidentiality for me. "Ummm, you're not supposed to violate your patient's privacy."

"She's not my patient. She's my best friend. Her foster mother pleaded with the court to have her daughter committed," Dr. Marcus told me. "Her foster mother felt guilty about all the things Londyn endured from the day your mother gave her up to the foster system. Londyn had been passed around through those men in that family until they got tired and basically sold her to the LePonts. I met her when we were in the sixth grade. Once she was married off to that family, the only time I got to see her was during visitation after she was committed. I got my doctorate degree specifically so I could work here as her psychiatrist. I knew I'd never see her again outside of this hospital. This way, I can see her every day if I choose."

I watched a tear slide down her face before she hurried up and wiped it. At least my sister had a friend. That gave me a little comfort. "I was here an entire year, and no one told me about her."

The doctor nodded. "Yes, it was best you didn't know she was here. She's in solitary. Well, sometimes. She has her ways of getting what she wants around here."

I wasn't even sure what to say except, "I don't even remember her. How long had it been since I'd seen her?"

"Your mother gave her up when she was about two. That's why you have no memory of her. She says you had a sister who's about a year and a half older than you. I think she says her name is Brielle. Do you remember Brielle?" The doctor looked me in the face.

"Barely," I whispered, my heart sinking in my chest.

"Oh, really?" Dr. Marcus scoffed. "According to the authorities who picked you up from Charlotte, they found you in Brielle's recovery room. She'd just lost a baby and had a hysterectomy. They said that she'd ingested something or possibly been drugged. Did you drug your sister?"

I looked at her like she'd lost her fuckin' mind. If security wasn't standing right outside her office door, I probably would have reached for the letter opener on her desk and jabbed it in her fuckin' neck.

"No, I didn't poison Brielle. She was trying to help me, and I fucked everything up for her. Everything she's worked hard for can be over, and it's because of me. My big sister lost a baby, and it could've been my fault. Not because I poisoned her but because I fucked with someone I shouldn't have. I knew better than to fuck with that lady's husband. I don't deserve to leave this place. I want to see my twin."

"I'll make sure a nurse's assistant takes you down to The Dungeon to see her tomorrow after the court date." The doctor watched my eyes widen. "It's what we call solitary here, hun, remember?"

I sighed in relief. "I forgot. I forgot a lot of things. I forgot my sister, my *twin* sister. I have a *twin* sister named Londyn! This is hilarious." I laughed to mask the pain. "Did she say why she killed those people?"

"You'll find out in court tomorrow, sweetie." Dr. Marcus smiled a little. "You're all that girl talks about."

The rest of the day was a blur. I blocked any and everything out that didn't have to do with my sister. I was desperate to meet her; I wanted to see her face again and know that I wasn't dreaming. There were so many questions that I had for her. I wanted to know how long she had known about me.

Upon entering the courtroom, I spotted Trap sitting behind the defendant's table with that dancer bitch. I knew it. I knew that bitch would sink her acrylic nails into my nigga as soon as she got the chance. The shit shouldn't have even hurt, but it did.

"Where is my sister?" I whispered to my lawyer as he led me to the defendant's table to sit down.

The lawyer, Dave Harris, nodded toward a flat-screen TV that hung in the corner of the courtroom.

My heart froze at the sight of my sister in a straight jacket, grinning into the camera. She was definitely a livelier version of myself. She had a head full of thick, dark, curly hair. My eyes were brown with specks of green, whereas her eyes were green with specks of brown. Her skin was flawless, almost as if she had frequent facials. She definitely didn't look like a mental patient, but that straight-jacket said otherwise. They had that muthafucka strapped up tightly, and she actually looked comfortable.

The judge came into the courtroom. I was staring so hard at my sister that Dave had to nudge me to get my attention so I could stand up. I snapped out of my trance, the whispers from the prosecution table catching my attention. I glanced to the left, rolling my eyes at the nurses that I was told I'd injured. Meredith still had the print from that lamp cord around her neck, and the left side of Lacy's face looked out of place. They both looked my way before shaking their heads in disgust. Those two bitches used to stand watch while my father would rape me. I hadn't seen my sister since I was a baby, and I had no memory of her, yet she came to my rescue when I needed someone most.

"Your honor," the state's attorney spoke up after the case was presented before the court. "Though Mrs. Gia Starr escaped the Bayou in November, she is not responsible for the deaths of officers Stanley Banks and Wilco Stevens. Nor is she responsible for the injuries that Lacy Danburry and Meredith March sustained. We originally charged Mrs. Gia Starr with these crimes, but with these witnesses' testimony and that of her sister, we will dismiss the charges."

The judge looked over her reading glasses at me, sitting nervously in my chair. "Mrs. Starr, do you remember any of the events that took place that night?"

My heart contracted rapidly in my chest. I tried to block the memory of my father raping me that afternoon from my mind, but as soon as she asked me if I remembered what had happened, my father's moans in my ear appeared in my mind. Lacy had given him a sedative to inject me with moments before. She gave him the drugs he needed to temporarily paralyze me that night. *That,* I did remember, but I was tired of talking about that muthafucka.

"No, I don't remember anything but waking up in a hospital," I stuttered, standing up from my seat.

"I remember everything from that night," Londyn spoke up, getting everyone's attention.

We all looked up at her as she sat up straight in her chair, smiling a little before she went on to tell her account of that night.

"I kicked that redhead bitch in her face with these Timberland boots that I stole from maintenance. She wouldn't go down, so I bashed her in her face with the lamp. The other nurse with the flat ass jumped on me, and I managed to wring her fuckin' neck with the lamp cord. These hoes were standing outside the door while Gia was being raped by her father. *Our* father. Yeah, I shot those fat fuckers who weren't securing shit but them Krispy Kreme donuts they stuffed their faces with. Our own father was fuckin' her, and security let him in. Those bitches were watching that shit through the glass!" Londyn squirmed in her seat as if she was trying to wiggle free from the straight jacket.

The judge looked over at me, watching me exhaling deeply, already knowing what her next question was going to be. "Have charges been placed against her father for these allegations?"

"Gia was having sex with a few of the staff members at the facility. For her to blame her father, a highly respected man from a prestigious—"

Londyn cut Meredith off. "You two watched that bastard drug and fuck his own daughter that night! *That's* why I beat your asses and killed the guards who let that nigga in!"

"Is-is there any proof of rape?" the judge hesitated to ask.

"The baby she has isn't proof enough?" Londyn scoffed. "Arrest that nigga! Put him in here so I can get to him, too! When I get my hands on him, I'm gonna do to him everything he did to my sister!"

My heart was speeding in my chest like a NASCAR driver. No one had ever risked their life to save mine. I didn't even remember her. What kind of sister was I? I'd fucked the husband of a person who was helping run my older sister's company. And I couldn't even remember my own twin fuckin' sister. She'd gotten away from my mother's abrasiveness, but I was sure her foster family made up for it in their ill treatment of her. Poor Londyn.

"Ain't no ocean, ain't no sea! Makidada! Keep my sister way from me!" Londyn laughed and sang as the judge banged her gavel.

"Ummm, George, contain your client over there!" The judge's pale skin was turning red as she watched my sister laugh hysterically.

"My sister was here an entire year before I found out she was in this muthafucka!" Londyn's laugh abruptly stopped, and her light eyes turned an even brighter green. Almost yellow. Like a black cat's eyes. "These bitches watched that cracker-ass-nigga rape my sister that night. I don't give a fuck what they tell you! The man they let into my sister's room was her own father! I'm sorry the security officers aren't here to tell you their side of their fucked-up story, and these two pasty bitches wanna lie because he probably paid them or they're family members or some shit. But they got what they deserved, and I'll do the shit again if they ever come the fuck near me! Go anywhere near my sister, and I promise you won't live to testify in court, you evil, swamp-pussy, split-end-having, trailer-park, I'm-not-racist-I-have-two-black-friends hoes!"

I was mesmerized by the sight of my sister kicking and

screaming as the medical staff at the Baltimore Bayou tried to get her out of the chair. The judge tried to over-talk my sister's screams as she dropped the case against me and charged my sister with two counts of assault and two counts of first-degree murder. She was confined to that mental institution for life. She was never getting out.

As promised, Dr. Marcus had one of the CNAs get me from my room and take me down to solitary. The CNA had to enter a five-digit code into a deadbolt lock to get into sis's room. The door clicked and opened. I'd been in solitary for months at a time and was in a room the size of a closet. They had Londyn in a room the size of a studio apartment.

"But a bitch can't get a dollar out of me. No Cadillacs, no perm, you can't see that I'm a muthafuckin' P-I-M-P!" I always liked that song, but hearing Londyn sing it in a voice sweeter than Jhene Aiko's was music to my ears.

Londyn sang while going through a mini-fridge that was stocked with every color and flavor of Jell-O you could think of. Not to mention gummy bears, cookies, and all sorts of snacks were in baskets on top of the fridge.

Londyn looked back at me and the CNA over her shoulder before digging back through her refrigerator. "Look, maintenance is about to come in here and fix my toilet in about an hour. I'm finna suck this nigga's dick from the back for a few cigarettes. Can we reschedule this visit?"

"Any sharp edges in here?" The CNA walked into the room, leaving me standing near the door in my gown. She wouldn't even let me wear the tennis shoes they'd given me because of the laces.

"No. Y'all took all my shit when I stabbed the nurse with a

fork." Londyn huffed. "Now I have to suck all this shit out of the cups. I appreciate the tongue exercises, though. I'm gonna need it for that new aerobics instructor. That bitch is bad. Did you see that ass, Ms. Wilma?"

The CNA rolled her big brown eyes as she walked around the room to do a quick inspection. "I'm only letting Geor'Gia in here as a favor to Dr. Marcus. She thinks it's time that you two meet face to face. I'll be back in an hour," Meredith told us as she looked under Londyn's mattress, eying a lighter, nail polish remover, scissors and duct tape. Not to mention a list of some kind. Wilma squinted, reading the paper out loud, then gasped in disbelief. "Isobel, Christina, Miranda—why are these CNAs listed on this piece of paper?"

Londyn grabbed a few cups of Jell-o before going over to sit on her recliner. "They wouldn't give me a razor so I could shave this hairy-ass pussy of mine. This shit looks like a magic carpet. They have until the day before my physical to get me a razor, or I'm taping them the fuck up, pouring nail polish remover on their hair, and lighting that shit."

Wilma crumpled the list and grabbed everything she'd found under the mattress. "You've been spitting out your meds. You *have* to swallow your meds."

"For what?" Londyn laughed, leaning back in the recliner. "I'm going to die in this muthafucka! You white muthafuckas get away with everything—"

"I'm black." Wilma pursed her lips.

"You white muthafuckas get away with everything," Londyn repeated. "I kill a few people who deserve to get fucked in the ass by Satan himself, and *I'm* in the wrong? Fuck *all* you hoes with a sick dick!"

"You wanna stay?" Wilma asked me, releasing an exhausted laugh like she was over my sister's bullshit.

I hesitated to nod, watching my sister lick Jell-O from her cup. "I wanna stay."

"One hour." Wilma approached me with my sister's things. "Please don't piss her off. I'd hate for her to try to drown you in her toilet like she did housekeeping the other night. Security is standing a few feet outside the door. If you need anything, just bang on the door."

I sighed heavily, watching her bang on the door with her free hand.

A few seconds later, the door snatched open, and Wilma let herself out.

I closed the door behind her and leaned against it while watching my sister sit up in her chair. I gulped before walking toward her. When I caught a glimpse of a picture taped to the wall above her nightstand, it stopped me in my tracks. I walked over to the nightstand to get a closer look. My eyes watered at the sight of myself, Londyn and Brielle sitting in these cute, fluffy dresses. Londyn and I couldn't have been older than a year and a half, and Brielle was just a year and a half older than we were. I couldn't tell Londyn and me apart in that picture.

"So, was Mama put in a casket, or was she air fried?" Londyn broke me from my trance.

I made a face, looking up at her from the picture. "Say what?"

"Did muthafuckas actually pay almost eight thousand dollars for her casket? When I die, just air fry my ass. So, did y'all air fry the bitch or what? It's not like she loved us. She gave me up when I was a toddler, and I heard she damn near beat you and Brielle to death before a muthafucka beat *her* to death." Londyn got up from her recliner and tossed the empty cup of jello into the trashcan next to her chair. "I was passed around by white men all my fuckin' life. Brielle was pimped out by her grandmother, and your white father taught you how to suck dick."

My nostrils flared as my sister walked up to me, baring our ugly truths.

"I saw our father walking out of this mental institution, lighting a cigar like he'd just accomplished something." Londyn approached me. "I went to your room and saw those nurses walking out, mentioning the fact that they'd sat you up in the corner of your room and that you'd regain feeling once the anesthesia they gave you wore off. The two security guards were joking about the screams they heard coming from your room. That bastard had everyone thinking you were his step-daughter and that you were having an affair with him. He made them sedate you because he told them he wanted to have sex with his girlfriend without the voices in your head screaming at you. And they believed him!"

Tears slid down my face. "He-he calls Fridays 'Freaky Fridays,'" I whispered. "As soon as I'd see his face, Gabby would start screaming at him. But as soon as he'd touch me, Megan would do whatever he said. Sometimes, Gabby would fight Megan. Whether I was coming on or going off my period depended on who would win. The birth control was the only thing that seemed to tame Megan.

"Once I was admitted to this place, Dad made sure they didn't put me on birth control, but once I got pregnant, Megan was gone. And Gabby would fight the muthafucka. My little girl was barely a week old when they started letting him back into the hospital. The sick bastard told me that he and his wife wanted another baby, but she couldn't have any kids. He was trying to get me pregnant again! I'd already lost two of his babies before! There I was, had just given birth to his third, and he was trying to get me pregnant again!"

Londyn's eyes turned that crazy yellow again, her pupils

almost non-existent. "Are you gonna kill that bitch-ass cracker when you get out of here? They're letting you go. Ain't you married to a rapper? I know that nigga has niggas! I heard you were in a group home; you ought to have some niggas from there, too! I know *I* do! One of them is about to be here in a few minutes! Niggas will do almost anything for pussy and money, sista, and I have both." Londyn laughed before turning around to walk away from me.

I dried my face, walking a few feet behind her. "Dr. Marcus told me about your family."

"You think I'm crazy for killing my mother-in-law?"

Londyn sat on her bed and waved for me to come over and sit beside her. She reached into her nightstand, pulling out a bottle of vanilla cashmere EOS lotion.

I shook my head. "We all have our breaking point."

"The bitch hated me, but she had me in her will because she hated her children even more." Londyn grinned. "The bitch left me nine million." She watched my eyes widen. "I'm a millionaire psychopath! They had that bitch cremated, and I don't even blame them. Makes no sense to spend bands to bury someone who was going straight to hell anyway. My in-laws were pissed when I didn't get the death sentence, *and* their mama left me all that money. The fact that they Easy-baked the bitch instead of having a funeral probably made them feel a little better. My husband filed for divorce the day I was put in this bitch. I've been in this bitch since I was eighteen. What good is all that money going to do for me in here?" Londyn's grin faded. "I'll never have any children. Never get married. Never fall in love."

"It's not all it's cracked up to be." I sighed heavily as I watched this beautiful sister, who I never even knew I had, rub lotion over her arms and legs. "I ruined everything. I lost my husband. I lost my best friend. I ruined my sister's life. I don't know how to fix any of this."

Londyn frowned at me as she rubbed lotion on her elbows. "You're a celebrity wife."

I laughed out loud. "That nigga showed up in court with his backup dancer! *She's* his 'celebrity wife!' I'm filing for divorce as soon as I leave here."

Londyn shook her head, putting her lotion back in the drawer. "Don't do that shit. You won't get shit in alimony, and if you do, there will be a fuckin' guardian over your money because of your mental history. Play nice with the nigga. Let him do his thing, and you do yours."

"Doing my thing is what got Brielle's baby killed!" I let Londyn know.

Londyn disagreed. "I'm sure big sista isn't clean either. Who's her baby daddy?"

"Shadow Shade." I watched Londyn snicker.

"Ouuu, that nigga isn't about to play. The Shade family, huh? How did she get mixed up with that family?" Londyn scoffed.

"She ain't the only one," I muttered.

Londyn looked up at me. "Well, there you go. There goes your crew right there. You're taken care of and don't even know it." Londyn looked up on the wall at the clock ticking loudly. "Well, if you don't mind, I gotta get ready for my dick appointment." She looked back at me.

My heart pounded in my chest. I wasn't ready to leave her just yet. I'd just found her. "I-I don't even remember having a twin, but I do remember feeling like a piece of me was missing."

Londyn huffed, getting off her bed. "Girl, I'm not trying to reminisce with you. I'm trying to reminisce with that ten-and-a-half-inch dick who's about to walk through that door."

"You defended me, and you barely knew me," I reminded her.

"I defended *me*," she snapped. "When I saw you on that floor in your room, I saw myself in the corner after my foster brothers would rape me. Nobody was there for me. Brielle became a real estate agent, you married a hip-hop superstar, and I ended up being sold to the highest bidder!" Londyn laughed out loud, running her hands through her curly hair.

"You fought for me, Londyn. And I thank you," I had to let her know.

"You're my sister. I'd go against anything that goes against you. Don't start that crying shit." She huffed, watching me start to cry. "Get the fuck out. You came, you saw, now you can go on with your life. *Fight* for your life. That's what I'd do if I could get those ten years back. Don't fuck it up."

I stood from her bed as she leaned back against the wall, looking straight ahead, her eyes glistening. "I need your help again."

She looked at me as I walked over to her.

"You want my life? It's yours," I told her.

Londyn laughed a little, her laughter subsiding when she realized by the look on my face that I wasn't joking. "The fuck is wrong with you?"

"We look damn near identical, except for that weird shit your eyes do when you get mad. And your hair is definitely thicker. Do you have any tattoos or anything?" I asked, and she pursed her lips.

"Right, because there are so many tattoo artists in a mental institution. Bitch, turn around, walk away, and don't look back." Londyn pushed past me.

"I'm not strong enough to be out there. You're my strength, Londyn!" I told her. "Please!"

Londyn stopped in her tracks.

"Do you know that I stayed in the room right next to this one for months and never knew you existed? It's time for you to exist again outside of this place, Londyn!" I yelled.

"Will you be okay here by yourself?" Londyn asked before turning around.

"They'll think I'm you." I watched Londyn look like she was actually contemplating what I was asking her to do. "I'll be fine. No worse than what I go through out there."

"Jaliyah, she'll know you're not me." Londyn hesitated.

"Jaliyah will be glad her friend is free." My eyes searched her face, wondering if she'd really take me up on my offer to free her.

"We have a lot of shit to go over. I don't know you, and you don't know me." Londyn exhaled deeply, still looking very unsure of the situation. "When are you getting out of here?"

I grinned a little. "You mean, when are *you* getting out of here?"

CHAPTER TWO
LONDYN

I hadn't seen the outside of that mental institution since I was eighteen fuckin' years old. The first thing I did when I got out was get some fuckin Wendy's. Did you know that you could get a junior bacon cheeseburger, fries, nuggets, *and* a drink for five dollars? Shit, I didn't. I sat alone, staring out the window of the restaurant in a daze. I was free. Well, free to be Gia.

We sat down that night after I let the maintenance man do some maintenance on my insides. Gia had a plan, and I had some plans of my own. The first order of business was having Jaliyah let me use her office phone the next morning to add Gia as an authorized user on my bank account so I could use it while I pretended to be her. I didn't tell Jaliyah my plan. She had no idea why I'd add a person I barely knew to my bank account, sister or not.

The bitch left me a check after I killed her. It had been almost ten years since I killed that old wrinkly hag, and I still couldn't wrap my mind around the fact that she'd left me money just to piss her family off. I laughed my ass off the day I was sentenced to life at the Baltimore Bayou, and my husband's family tried to not just attack me but the judge who gave me the sentence.

The moment I walked out of the Baltimore Bayou after nine years, I laughed that same hysterical laugh. Gia and I switched places the night before she was supposed to be released, and the nursing staff didn't even fuckin' notice. Gia told me not to ever come back, to leave her in that place. I wasn't going to leave her; I was just going to help her straighten up a few things.

"Oh, my goodness!" A dark-skinned chick with cornrows stopped abruptly at the table I was sitting at. "It's Gia Starr!"

I looked up at her, rolling my eyes a little before taking a sip of my strawberry lemonade. "Oh, yeah, I'm Gia," I mumbled to myself before looking up at the bitch and faking a smile. "Do you want an autograph or something?"

Her smile quickly faded. "Nah, I'm Kevia. Your children's nanny. I work for your husband."

I just stared up at her, waiting for her to say something that might actually have meant a damn thing to me. "And?"

"*And* he's about to go on tour tomorrow night. He's staying at the Hilton with Odyssey, his backup dancer," Kevia said in disgust as she watched me chew on my fries.

I didn't give a fuck about Trap. Gia told me to get back to Charlotte and figure out how the fuck the cops found her in the first place. Her children needed to be out of harm's way. News had already spread that she was spotted coming out of a mental institution. I was sure that whoever put her in the muthafucka would try to figure out sooner or later why she'd gotten out. Sis didn't want to tell me that she was involved with Knight Shade, an old *married* friend whom she knew from when she was in a group home. If he was anything like she'd described, he was already looking for her and the person who put her there. Not to mention, his older brother, Shadow, was probably after who'd poisoned Big Sis and killed their baby. I had my eye on Marley, Knight's wife, but I had a feeling it was deeper than that. I didn't have time to worry about what the fuck Trap was doing with his side bitch.

"I don't give a fuck about his new bitch." I huffed, dipping my fries in a pack of sweet and sour sauce. "He can fuck her on stage for all I give a fuck. I'm heading back to Charlotte. And since you're the nanny, where the fuck are my kids?"

"They're with his mama at the hotel," Kevia hesitated to say. "The night before your court date, I walked in on Odyssey, smacking Nephy in the face."

My eye twitched. I was trying my best not to lose my cool. "Omarion did what to my baby?"

With tears in her eyes, she laughed out loud at me purposely messing up the bitch's name. "The babies are with your mother-in-law in room 416, and your husband is across the hall in 417. I know I'll be out of a job, but that woman doesn't need to be around your kids. Trap doesn't know what type of woman she is. He just sees all that ass. I mean, you've seen it. It's a nice ass. That's all a grieving man sees. You didn't die, but you've been gone a long time. He hasn't been the same since you went away. I just thought you should know."

"Yeah, whatever. Can you get me an Uber? I caught a cab here from The Bayou. I don't exactly have a phone, or luggage for that matter. I haven't shaved my pussy in months, and I'm wearing scrubs that one of the CNAs gave me." I tapped my foot anxiously as Kevia went through her pocket to grab her phone.

I don't know when the last time I'd been in the backseat of a car without one of my foster family members trying to feel me up. The Uber driver kept looking back at me like he wanted to ask me if I was really my sister, but he didn't. He barely pulled up at the curb of the hotel before I hopped out of the car. Gia told me to forget about that nigga and go see about her sister, but her kids. She thought she was better off without her kids, that she didn't deserve them, but I knew her heart. Shit, it was the other half of mine.

I was told I could never have children. They said my ovaries stopped producing eggs when I was about twelve as a result of sexual abuse. I was supposed to be Gia; therefore, her kids were mine, and I was going to protect them.

Kevia wasn't lying; Omarion had an ass so fat that you could see from the front. She stood at the hotel room door in shock for a few seconds before her attitude sank in.

"How the fuck did you get past security? We don't need any towels." Omarion rolled her neck at me, a slight grin on her face.

"Bitch, what?" I asked.

"Babe, who is it?" Trap's voice surfaced from the bathroom down the hallway.

"Oh, it's just the help, asking us if we need any towels. But we're good, right?" Omarion looked over her shoulder. She barely got to look back at me with that stupid grin on her face before I popped her right in her fuckin' mouth.

She stumbled back, and I pushed my way inside. I was sitting on that bitch's chest, hands wrapped tightly around her throat. I smiled at her, showing the blade I had clenched between my teeth when Trap came running out of the bathroom toward us. I'm not even sure how he did it, but he came behind me and gently yet firmly pulled me off the girl. The warmth of his embrace caused me to let go of Omarion's neck.

The bitch was gasping for air, yet she got off the floor, trying to charge at me, when Trap grabbed her and threw her against the wall as if *she* was the one who'd attacked me. His actions didn't prove the things my sister said about him at all.

He loved Gia, alright. All that ass on Omarion didn't mean shit when he saw her attempting to fight me back. He hadn't even heard why I was about to slit her throat from ear to ear, and he was already defending me.

"Nigga!" Omarion rubbed her neck with one hand and shoved Trap with the other. "The patient tried to choke me, and you're pushing *me* into a wall?"

"'The help with towels'? Is that what you just called her?" Trap's thick eyebrows frowned as he looked down into the dancer's face.

Omarion scoffed before looking at me standing behind him, removing the razor from my teeth. She looked back at Trap. "That's the same woman who tried to poison your son! Who had a baby by a nigga at the psych ward! But you're right. I shouldn't have called her the help. What I should have called her was the bitch who should've stayed at the psych ward! She shouldn't even be out! Put the bitch back in there and throw away the fuckin' key!"

I laughed out loud. "Says the bitch who the nanny caught hitting Gia's little boy."

Trap looked back over his shoulder at me. Gia said that people in her life were used to her referring to herself in the third person, especially when she was having one of her psychotic episodes. So, if I slipped up every once in a while and forgot that I was supposed to be playing her part, no one would think anything of it.

"You hit my fuckin' son!" I corrected myself.

"You tried to poison him!" Omarion yelled back at me.

Trap backed her into the wall. "Hold up. She's telling the truth? You hit my son?"

The anger in Omarion's voice quickly subsided, and fear took over. She looked into Trap's face remorsefully, more like the look of a scared dog. "He wouldn't stop crying!" Omarion started crying like most bitches did.

"He's seventeen months old! He's a fuckin' baby! What else do babies do?" Trap yelled in her face, pushing past her.

"Trap, please!" Omarion pleaded, chasing behind him. She was wearing one of his t-shirts and no panties. That thang was definitely thangin'.

"Yo, you better get away from me, Odyssey, before I let my wife tag that ass," Trap growled at her.

I leaned against the wall, giggling to myself at the sound of zippers and what sounded like a suitcase rolling. I looked up to see Trap wheeling a suitcase from the room. Omarion chased behind him, crying, pleading, and screaming. Trap did not give a fuck. He opened the door to the hotel room and tossed her suitcase out before tossing her sexy chocolate ass out on her ass, closing the door behind her. Trap then went over to the minibar, grabbed a bottle of Hennessy, and unscrewed the top.

I approached him as he sat on the sofa. Omarion was still banging on the door. A few seconds later, male voices were outside of the door. Omarion's voice faded as if she was being dragged away from the door.

"Security is in the room next door," Trap let me know before taking a few long gulps from his bottle. "Mama took the kids with her to get a nigga some soul food from somewhere. Who told you Odyssey hit my son?"

"Your nanny." I sat down beside him.

"He hasn't seen you since he was five months old, but I show him your picture whenever I can. I can tell he misses you." Trap glanced at me before taking another gulp of liquor. "I miss you, too."

I rolled my eyes a little and grabbed the bottle from him. "You put me in that fuckin' place, Travis."

Trap laughed a little. "This is new, calling me by my government." He watched me drink the brown substance like it was water. "I was trying to help you. I love you, and at one time, you loved me. I put you in that place to get you some help. I hired a private investigator to look for you once I found out you escaped."

I looked at him, lowering the bottle from my lips. "Private investigator?"

Trap nodded. "He was supposed to bring you to me first. Whatever made him call the police to come get you first, I'm not sure. It wasn't until I got the call from the lawyer that you were back at The Bayou that I found out you had a twin sister. A twin sister who admitted to taking out staff members to protect you. They took your baby girl to the nursery. They were just about to call your so-called stepfather to come get her when I got there. I can't believe this bitch was hitting my baby."

"Nigga, how long have you been hittin' *her*?" I asked, turning to him. "How long have you been fuckin' Omarion?"

Trap made a face. "The fuck are you talkin' about?"

"That bitch you just threw out of here!" I shoved the bottle into his chest. I hated cheating-ass niggas, mine or not. "How long have you been fuckin' her? Was it before you just threw me away?"

Trap shook his head. "I didn't 'just throw you away.'"

"Do you have any idea of the things I've gone through in that place? Of the shit I went through *before* I went into that place? The Bayou is Disney World compared to my life before I went there!" I laughed, getting up from the couch. "My sister did what she did for me because no daughter should have to lose her virginity to her own fuckin' father! We never got a choice; everything was chosen for us! We'd been separated since we were toddlers and still managed to live the same fuckin' life!" I pulled my scrubs shirt over my head and tossed it at his face.

Trap snatched my shirt from his head, his eyes tracing my breasts. He stood from the sofa and tossed the shirt down before grabbing my wrist. "What are you doing?"

"I need a fuckin' shower. I need to get out of these clothes. I need to get on the bus and head back to Charlotte to clean up the mess she made." I looked into his face as I snatched away from him. "We made a mess. Me and my older sister, Brielle, made a mess. That's all I'm doing. I only came here to tell your bitch to keep her hands off those kids who are small and defenseless and who didn't ask to fuckin' be here! Why did you let this bitch around my kids?"

Trap was still stuck on my titties, too shook to answer my question.

I mushed him in his head. "Then you brought that bitch to court. Bitch probably got that lace front from Wish."

"These hoes shop at Shein. You haven't been in that mental institution that long, mamas." Trap frowned.

"Well, wherever the fuck she got it from, nigga. What's under that wig? I bet Omarion looks like a handsome boy underneath that shit. If I catch her around you after I just told you she put her hands on our son, I will give her a hysterectomy myself. If you don't want me to gut that bitch in front of you, you better stay the fuck away from her. Don't let me see that bitch on stage dancing, or I'm gonna dance on her fuckin' face." I pulled the straps to my pants, letting them fall to my ankles before I stepped out of them. "Where's the got-damn soap? And it better be Dove Sensitive." I walked away from the couch toward the bathroom.

"Do you remember the day we got married?" Trap called out to me.

I stopped in the hallway, turning around to face him as he walked toward me. "Nigga, what?"

Trap unhooked a chain around his neck that had a wedding band and engagement ring hanging from it. "You were scared as fuck of a big wedding. Said you wanted it to just be you and me. You even let a nigga pick out your dress." Trap laughed a little, walking up to me and grabbing me by the hand. He placed that cold chain in my hand.

I was standing there, naked as fuck, and he wanted to talk about a corny ass wedding day. He looked into my face, grinning a little at the thought of the day that my sister probably didn't even remember.

"I got the magistrate to let a nigga play 'For However Long' on my phone as you walked toward me. And the bailiff put my phone in front of the microphone so the entire courtroom could hear that shit loud and clear. We were just two kids getting married straight out of fuckin' high school. I had just signed a recording deal with Trap Soul Records, and my manager was telling me that I was making a mistake by marrying you. I thought so, too, until the day you walked into that courtroom in that short beige dress and your dark hair straightened, flowing down your back. All I could think about was, 'That's mine right there.'" Trap sighed to himself, taking the chain from my hands and sliding the platinum wedding ring set from it.

I tried to pull away from him, but he grabbed my left hand, sliding the rings onto my ring finger.

"You threw these rings back at me the day I put you in the Baltimore Bayou. You said you never wanted to see me again." He frowned down into my face.

I frowned back before I looked down at his hand and noticed that the nigga was wearing his wedding band. Gia mentioned the night before that he wasn't wearing it the day she was cuffed to the hospital bed, but there he was, wearing that shit proudly.

"Nigga, you fuckin' bitches with your wedding ring on?"

I could barely look back into the nigga's face before he grabbed my body to his and kissed my lips. I shoved him into the wall, attempting to wipe his kiss from my lips, when he grabbed me again, backing me into the opposite wall and kissing me once more.

The anger I was supposed to feel for him putting my sister away when she needed him most quickly disappeared. I felt love. I felt affection. I felt craved. Have you ever felt craved? Not lusted after, but craved? He kissed me against that wall like his very life depended on it, and mine too. Yeah, I'd fucked a few of the CNAs and MTs at the Bayou for favors. I was lusted after by the men on the staff. I could get anything I wanted. But the way that Trap sucked on my lips that day made me want to give *him* anything he wanted. But, no, he was my sister's nigga.

"No, nigga, get off me." I shoved him off me. "My pussy is hairy as fuck. I ain't fuckin' with you. Give me the soap so I can shower. Take ya ring back and give it to Omarion." I started to pull his rings off when he grabbed me by the neck.

I gasped and giggled in delight. He was about to activate something in me that he wasn't ready for. He was dressed in a white tank top and boxers; I saw that dick swinging moments earlier when he was throwing Omarion out of the room.

"You don't know what you're about to unleash, Travis. You better let go of my neck." And the nigga gripped it tighter. I could feel my pupils dilating.

"Gia, you have my last name. You are mine. Do you hear me?" Trap growled at me. "We've been all over the world together. My first single was about you. You gave me my first child. You are the only woman who can take all this dick without running. You think I'm gonna let that go? Yeah, I've fucked a few hoes while you were away, but they will never amount to you, Gia. Yeah, you're a crazy bitch, but you're *my* crazy bitch."

"I want a fuckin' divorce," I hissed at him, nostrils flaring, his warm hands around my neck. That shit felt so good. I felt a few drops of wetness dripping down my thigh.

"'Til death do we fuckin' part, Gia." He let go of my neck and watched me pretend like I wasn't gasping for air. "On our wedding day, in front of God and in front of that magistrate, you promised me... you. I didn't throw you to the wolves. I put you in a place where you couldn't hurt your children or yourself. I gave you the space I thought you needed when maybe I should've held you and told you I wasn't going anywhere. I fucked up, and I want my wife back."

"I don't feel like a fuckin' wife." I sighed heavily, still feeling the warmth of his hand around my neck.

"Well, maybe that's because I haven't been much of a husband." He slid his hands around my neck and up through my fuckin' hair, gripping it in his hands as he pulled my face to his. "Forgive me, please." His lips caressed mine.

"No." I pulled my lips from his. "She doesn't want me to forgive you!" I shoved him in his chest.

Trap frowned, looking into my face, probably trying to figure out which 'she' I was referring to."

"Londyn was there!" I tried to clean up what I'd just said. "She was there, and you weren't! Why should I forgive you?"

I tried to remain calm as he grabbed my hand and slid it down his boxers. My mouth gaped open as I looked up into his face. My hand slid for what felt like miles down his erection. The veins on that fat nigga felt like a road map.

"He misses you." Trap grinned a little.

"He..." I gulped, at a loss for words for a second or two. "He has emotions, huh? I bet he talks, too. "

Trap agreed. "He's saying, 'Now go get in that bed and bend the fuck over.'"

I shook my head. I never fucked anyone at The Bayou without a condom. I can't tell you the number of times my foster family members had given me trich and chlamydia when I was younger. I didn't want that skin-to-skin contact. My ex-husband was drunk every time we had sex. He was too drunk to realize I'd never even sucked his dick without a flavored condom, let alone fucked him without one.

"Do you have a condom? No ticket, no skates, nigga," I told him.

The muthafucka looked at me like I'd just told him I was cutting off all that pretty hair of his. "You're my wife. I fucked those other bitches with condoms. I fuck you skin to skin. Come on, stop playing." He grabbed me by my hand, leading me into the bedroom.

I wanted to chicken out and tell the muthafucka that I was Londyn Cameron-LePont. That Gia was afraid to face everyone. That I was trying to help her clean everything up before switching back. That I'd been locked away for nine years. That I'd never been touched the way he was touching me. That I'd been in hell since I was two years old, and there it was, twenty-five years later, that I finally felt free.

I wasn't even supposed to be there with him. I was supposed to be making my way to Charlotte to check on Brielle and find out what happened to her baby. She'd had a hysterectomy and a miscarriage all in the same day. *That's* what I was supposed to be focused on. Not repairing a marriage that Gia obviously cared nothing about. She was in love with that nigga, Knight, and I couldn't figure out why when she had a man like Trap, who obviously still cared about her.

I slid my hand from his and circled back to the bathroom. "I need a shower."

Trying to get away from him, at least for a few minutes, I went into the bathroom and opened the frosted glass door to turn on the water. His cell phone lay on the counter, playing what sounded like music from my playlist. Music Jaliyah would let me listen to when I went into her office on Tuesdays and Thursdays. I barely got the chance to step into the shower when I felt him step inside with me. I gasped, turning around and eying the disposable razor in his hand before looking down at that dick swaying between his legs like a church bell.

Trap backed me into the shower, closing the door behind him. "You're running from me already? You've never run from me."

That bitch could take all that dick without running? I thought. *My bitch!* I grinned a little at the thought before shaking my head. "No, I'm not running. I haven't had a shower, and I need to—"

Trap lifted my left leg, resting my foot on the wood shower bench. "Come here. Let me shave that pussy."

I eyed the Eco shave gel, which lay in an indentation on the wall. "Omarion left her shaving cream, huh?" I rolled my eyes, watching him put shaving cream in his hands.

"Why the fuck did you pick Charlotte, North Carolina, of all places to run to after you escaped The Bayou?" Trap avoided the question by asking me another one.

I hesitated as he spread the cream all over my pussy. He made sure every hair on my pussy and my crack was covered in shave gel. "Wh-what do you mean?" I looked into his face.

"You never told me you had any sisters. According to the investigator, you had your sister Brielle thinking I beat the fuck out of you. He said your sister is running a program called SAFE for domestic violence survivors. The Shade family helps her run the organization." Trap looked irritated when he mentioned the family.

"And?" I tried to control my hormones as he started to shave in the direction my hair was growing.

Trap glanced at my face before looking back down at the area he was shaving. "Your bruises healed nicely. The ones you told your sister and the doctors at Shady Medical that I'd put on you. The only reason Knight didn't call was because of that program. They were trying to protect you from me, not knowing you needed protection from yourself. Knight figured it out when he started calling around after you had a psychotic break. He'd never met Megan or Gabby. You were on meds when you met him. I met Megan and Gabby the night we got married."

I gasped as he spread my lips apart to get a closer shave. "And-and you weren't scared?" My breath hitched.

"Nah." Trap shook his head. "I knew how to quiet them. I'm sure that nigga had to give you meds to make them stop yelling at you. All I had to do was talk to them, and they'd listen to me." He tilted his head, eying my pussy lips as he shaved the hair from her. "You know the nigga married your roommate from Wake Hills, Marley?"

I looked him in the face. "Marley?" I pretended to be familiar with her name, but not too familiar.

Gia told me all about the bitch. About how Marley found out she'd been fuckin Knight. Shit, about how Marley caught her riding the nigga's face in their house. Trap didn't need to know Gia was fuckin' Knight, nor did he need to know Marley had beef with Gia because of that shit.

"The crazy part is, during our last phone call, the private investigator FaceTimed me. He was sitting at his computer table, letting me know that the woman in his bed spotted you at her place with her nigga. And guess who the woman in his bed was?" Trap laughed a little. You know, that calm laugh right before a storm.

I looked up into Trap's face, heart speeding up as he stopped shaving my pussy and rinsed the razor under the shower head. I shook my head, realizing it was Marley who gave my sister up. Who the fuck was this investigator was what I wanted to know. Marley was at my sister's fuckin' neck over Knight, and she was fuckin' around on her nigga, too. The bitch was so slow, not even realizing that the investigator was probably only fuckin' her to get information on my sister.

"So, you ran to Charlotte to be with Knight? You were fuckin' Knight?" Trap's laughter subsided as he tossed the razor into the indentation on the shower wall.

I shook my head, looking him dead in the face. "Nah, not me. That was Gabby. Guess he figured out how to make the bitch shut up, too."

Trap looked down at me like he wanted to wring my fuckin' neck. He smiled a little. "Turn around and grab the bench."

I looked down at the peanut butter pole swinging between his legs. Before I could look into his face again and talk back to the nigga, he was turning me around, hands gripping my hips. He bent me over, his thumbs pressing into the small of my back. His fuckin' hands on my skin felt so good. His touch alone was amazing. I felt every emotion he was feeling through his touch. He was angry with Gia, but he knew he'd fucked up when he put Gia in that place. He thought she'd run to Charlotte looking for Knight when she had no idea the nigga was even there.

I gripped the back of the bench, arching my back deeper, feet shoulder-width apart. I looked back at him, grinning a little. I knew the nigga didn't think I was scared. My mama didn't raise me, but if she had, I was sure she wouldn't have raised no bitch. I'd been through more than a big ass dick. I'd never seen one that big. I was sure I could handle that shit, but maybe I should've done some stretches or something before I let the nigga stretch me the fuck out.

"Yeah, hold that ass just like that," he told me, holding my waist with his left hand and stroking his dick with his right a little before he led it through my pussy lips to find my opening. "When I fuck you, you better fuck me back. One band, one fuckin' sound. Ya feel me?"

I wanted to say something smart back to him, but the moment his dick filled me to the brim, I was immediately fuckin' speechless. I gripped the bench in my hands. If it would've been made of paper, that shit would've crumbled in my hands. I wanted to yell out *got-damn*, but I couldn't say a word. He was balls-deep in my pussy.

"With your permission..." Trap sang along with Ro James. "There's a whole lot of muthafuckin' lovin' that's way past due." He laughed a little since my legs had started shaking, and he hadn't even started stroking yet. "Pussy so tight feels like she's suckin' my dick. Got damn. Did you miss me?" he growled.

I didn't respond; I was still trying to hold my position.

"You don't hear me fuckin' talkin' to you? Answer your fuckin' husband." He gripped my hips as he put one foot on the stool.

I bit my lip as he stroked my pussy to the beat of the music. Once I caught the rhythm, I started to fuck him back as he'd asked me to do moments before.

That nigga had me wanting to yell out, "What's it gonna be? Cuz I can't pretend," like I was auditioning to sing backup for En Vogue. Gia didn't tell me she was married to Super Dick. Trap's dick had me feeling ways I never knew I hadn't felt. "Yes, I missed this dick." I exhaled heavily, speaking for my sister.

I understood that she was mad at him for dumping her off,

but who could stay mad at a dick like that? I was clinically insane as far as medicine was concerned, but I knew good dick when I felt it. It was the sweetest thing I'd ever known. That bitch was crazy, certified.

"How much?" Trap leaned forward, hand pressed against the wall, as he caused me to deepen my arch. "Enough to be home when I get back? Enough to stay away from Knight Shade?"

Though my knees wanted to buckle under me, I held my arch, taking every inch of him with ease. I didn't dare make a sound. I didn't want him to know how good he felt to me. A part of me felt guilty as fuck for what I was doing. I wasn't supposed to still be in Maryland. I was supposed to have been on that bus headed toward North Carolina. I wasn't supposed to be fuckin' my sister's husband; I wasn't even supposed to be anywhere near him. He was nowhere in our plan to get back at the muthafuckas who killed our sister's baby or who tried to have Gia thrown away for life.

When I wasn't moaning or screaming the way Trap wanted me to, he pulled out of me before turning my body around to face his. He lifted me, wrapping my legs around his waist. Then he reached behind us, turning off the shower before opening the door and stepping out. He carried me to the bedroom, kissing my lips along the way.

"You can't stay mad at me forever, mamas," he whispered, laying me down on the thick comforter. "I love you."

I shook my head as his body hovered over mine. I sighed, feeling his dick sliding up my thigh and between my legs. "Don't love me, okay?" I whispered, but he wasn't listening. "Take it back. Don't tell me you love me, please!"

There he was again, digging into my soul. He wrapped his arms around me, pulling my body into his. He dug into my pussy, grinding his pelvis against mine. I couldn't help but grind back. I couldn't hold back the moans any longer. He was fuckin' the shit out of me, and I was fuckin' the shit out of him. He bit my neck to muffle his moans.

"Thank you!" I didn't know what else to say. That shit had me thanking a nigga for his service.

Trap chuckled and kissed my neck. "Thank you, too, for your cervix." He held me tight, rolling over so I was on top. He held my hips, watching me sit up.

I panted, grinning a little before turning around on his dick, straddling his hips, and grabbing his thighs.

"Oh, you gonna ride my shit backward?" Trap smacked my ass before spreading it open. "Look at that shit... Even your asshole is pretty."

I sighed as he ran his hands over my ass before he gripped both cheeks. I started to wind my hips, giving him a little lap dance before I propped myself up on both feet and started bouncing on his dick.

"*Fuck!*" he yelled, gripping my waist.

"Put your thumb in my ass, husband." I looked back at him, moaning deeply as he did exactly what I said.

"You've never let me get anywhere near your ass before." Trap dug his thumb into my butt as he started fucking me from the bottom.

I bounced my ass, matching his thrusts. "Put your dick in my ass. Can you do that for me?" I attempted to stop riding his dick, but Trap sat up, holding me around my waist. I didn't know how he managed to get me on my stomach from that position, but he did, and quickly. "Spit in my asshole, daddy," I growled at him, looking over my shoulder as he pulled out of my pussy. I gasped as I felt a huge wad of spit dripping between my ass cheeks. I grabbed the sheets in my hands as I braced myself for impact.

Trap got the head of his dick into my asshole before spitting more saliva into my ass crack to create more lubrication. The nigga grabbed my neck with both hands, sending my emotions skyrocketing as he eased his way into my rectum. The shit hurt so good. I guess he was expecting me to just lay there, scared. Nah, I tooted my ass up to the sky, pumping back. I pushed my weight onto him, lifting from the bed and resting on my forearms.

Trap grabbed a hold of my waist as I threw it back. He moaned, and I moaned with him. I tried to match his thrusts until I couldn't take it anymore. I screamed, falling back onto the bed and letting him grind in me until he dumped globs of semen inside me. I grabbed the blanket with my teeth, toes curling as he continued to pump until his dick went semi-soft. His weight fell completely on top of me, and we both just lay there, panting.

I could still hear his phone playing in the bathroom down the hallway.

"I feel a little rush. I think I got a little crush on you. I hope it's not too much." Trap and I both whispered the lyrics to one of my favorite songs.

"You still love that song?" Trap kissed my neck before pulling out of me.

My sister and I had never been around each other, yet we had similar tastes in music. And Trap had that girl's playlist on his phone like it was his own. He studied that girl. I'd never experienced love, but if I had, I'd want it to be like that. Trap's little acts of kindness instantly gave my cold heart a rush. Liking the same music was a love language that I didn't even realize I spoke until that song played on that nigga's phone. I felt an instant soul connection.

I hesitated, lying on the bed to catch my breath. That song had come out a year after I'd been at The Bayou. Jaliyah played it for me one day in her office, and it had been stuck in my head ever since.

"You staying the night? Or are you going?" Trap got up from the bed, making his way toward the bathroom.

Before I could answer, there was a light tapping on the door.

"Who the fuck is it?" Trap called out from the bathroom.

"Nigga, it's ya mama!" a woman with a deep Southern accent called through the door.

CHAPTER THREE
LONDYN

My heart jumped in my chest as I sat up in bed, looking at the oversized chair in the corner of the room. A white t-shirt that I assumed he must've taken off earlier was draped across the back of the chair. I got up and grabbed the shirt, pulling it over my head. Then, I walked out of the room, eyeing Trap as he slipped into his boxers and made his way toward the hotel room door.

Trap barely got the door open when this pretty, brown-skinned woman pushed her way inside the hotel room. She couldn't have been much older than us. She definitely didn't dress like anyone's mama. It was the dead of winter, and she had on a crop-top hoodie and high-waisted leggings. She barged into the hotel, holding a car seat in one hand, with a little boy who looked like he'd just started walking following her. The little boy looked at me in admiration as he walked into the room. I'd never seen a cuter little boy. It was like God took the best parts of my sister and Trap and put them into that little boy. I walked toward them to get a glimpse of the baby in the car seat when shawty glared at me in disgust.

"Oh, the crazy bitch is back." She sneered at me as Trap closed the hotel room door behind her. "I told security not to let this bitch anywhere near you. They really let this bitch out of her cage?"

The little baby boy tried to make his way toward me, but the woman snatched him back.

"No!" he cried, trying to pull away.

Trap huffed, picking the little boy up in his arms. "Moms, don't call her that in front of our kids. The fuck is wrong with you?" He walked toward me with the little boy.

I backed up a little, almost backing into the couch behind me.

The little boy reached for me before Trap even got to me.

I sighed heavily as the little boy pretty much jumped out of Trap's arms and into mine. I was at a loss for words, forgetting what Gia said my little nephew's name was. He tugged at my curls as he looked into my face with wonder. After a few seconds, he reached back for Trap.

Trap noticed the hurt look on my face as he took his son from my arms. "It's been a minute since Nephy has seen you. Gotta give him a minute."

Trap's mother walked over to the couch and placed the car seat on the sofa adjacent to the one I was standing in front of. She faced me, crossing her arms as she stood in front of the car seat so I couldn't even get a glimpse of the baby. A gold and diamond Cuban link wrapped around her neck with a diamond encrusted *Katrina* charm dangling from it.

"I thought The Bayou said you were breastfeeding? Titties look kinda small to me." Katrina huffed, rolling her neck after every word she uttered.

Trap glanced at me and frowned, waiting for my response. He was so wrapped up in missing me that he probably didn't even realize my breasts definitely didn't look like I was nursing.

I shook my head. "I haven't been pumping for almost a month. The nurses at that place never have a fuckin' clue. You should know better than to listen to them, Katrina."

Katrina made a face at me. "Nah, I know better than to listen to *you*. As soon as you gave birth to a second child, they should have called me to come get this baby from you. I can't believe Trap was visiting you at that place when I *specifically* told the nigga not to." She frowned at her son as he sat on the couch behind me.

I looked back at Trap. He hadn't told his mother the baby wasn't his. He didn't even tell her that he hadn't been visiting Gia at The Bayou. He had her thinking the baby was his. That nigga really did love that girl. I wasn't sure why he didn't feel that I wasn't his wife; maybe because it had been so long since he'd been around Gia. He should have felt the difference between me and her. She said she met him when she was sixteen. He'd known her for eleven years. He should've noticed I wasn't Gia, identical twins or not. Gia and I had a lot in common despite being raised apart, but he should've known the difference, shouldn't he?

"She's my wife," Trap tried to tell her.

"And these are your kids. Your job is to protect them!" his mama snapped.

"My job is to protect *her*, their mother. She got the help she needed, and she's home now," Trap told his mother.

Katrina looked at me, pursing her lips. "Mmmhmm. You leaving?"

I hesitated to nod. "I'm going to Charlotte in the morning. I have some unfinished business to attend to."

I barely got the words out when Trap yanked my wrist to

pull me back down to the couch. I looked at him and pulled away.

Trap frowned, his eyes searching mine. "You're not staying in Maryland?"

"For what?" I scoffed. "Aren't you going on tour? I'm going to see my sister. She just lost her baby. She needs me. You obviously don't. Go on tour. Live your life the way you've been doing, Travis." I looked back at his mother. "Give me my baby."

"You're not taking my grandbabies with you, I know that. I will take this bitch to court for custody, and you know I'll win, Junior!" Katrina yelled at us.

Trap shook his head, his temples twitching. "Moms, chill out."

I glanced over toward the door, where I'd dropped the blade I was about to cut Omarion with. She had one more time to say something crazy, and I was going to slice her tongue out in front of her son and those beautiful kids.

"My kids are used to being around their grandmother, Trap. It's cool. You know old, wrinkled ladies love being around the youngins. It makes her feel young again at her old age." I laughed a little before the bitch had the nerve to step to me. I quickly stood from the couch.

Trap stood up, too, probably remembering what I'd just done to his groupie a little while ago. My asshole was still spasming from what that nigga had done to it; I didn't have time to go back and forth with his fuckin' mama.

"Little girl, keep trying me." Katrina pointed her finger in my face as her son backed her away from me. "You will *never* see these kids again!"

"Keep trying me, and you will never *see* again," I warned her, feeling the blood start to sprint through my veins. When I got mad, I craved the sight of blood or the sound of bones cracking. One wrong move, and I was going to peel her fuckin' face off.

"Mama, come on. You're not about to keep disrespecting her. You are the guardian of my kids when I'm on tour. That's it. She is their mother indefinitely. She gave birth to those kids, not you. Back the fuck up." Trap put some distance between me and his mother.

Katrina pushed his hand away after he backed her up a few feet to the other couch. "Nigga, I have raised that little boy for thirteen months! He's going on eighteen months old! I've had him since he was five months old! I was there when his first two teeth grew in! I was there when he started crawling! I was there when he started walking! I'm there to hold him when he's crying! I was there for his first Christmas! I take him to church with me every fuckin' Sunday, got damn it!" She shoved her son in his chest. "Everything I missed with you, I made up for with him. And I won't let her take that away from me!"

My anger subsided a little as I watched the pain seep into Trap's face. I had no idea what he'd gone through with that woman, but whatever he'd experienced with her was hurting him at that moment. Gia hadn't told me anything about Trap other than that he was friends with Knight at one point and that their fathers were both pastors.

"If you can't learn to get along with Gia, I'm going to get my lawyer to appoint the nanny as guardian." Trap watched his mother gasp. "When I get back from tour, I'm going to help you look for a place."

Katrina laughed out loud. "You're kicking me out of your house? For her? After all she's put you through, why do you still love her?"

Trap looked back at me before looking his mother in her face. "She's always seen me for who I am and not what I've been through. She was there for me when you weren't. My father was the pastor of the church we attended. He never acknowledged me. I hung around the wrong crowd. My ways sent my homeboy, Knight, to a group home. He took the fall for me, and I ended up at the same group home a few months later. I knew he was in love with Gia the day he introduced me to her, but... I was in pain until I met her. I had to have her. She was mine when I met her, and she's mine now. You don't like that I love her, and I don't give a fuck. She is my wife, and she always will be."

"She's a mistake, son." Katrina's big brown eyes watered.

"Well, she's *my* mistake to make, not yours," Trap told his mother as she pushed past him.

Katrina stopped to glare at me before walking around me to get Nephy off the sofa. "The kids are tired. They need to lie down. The baby just fell asleep after fussing. We'll see you at the airport in the morning, Trap."

I eyed Nephy as Katrina walked by me, holding him tightly in her arms as if she were afraid I would snatch him from her. I could tell by the way she held onto my nephew that she really did love him. That she really needed him. I saw then why Gia felt so guilty about everything she felt she'd done in Charlotte. She had an entire family waiting for her in Maryland.

I could tell by the look on Trap's face as he watched his mother leave with those kids that he really didn't want to leave his children or me. Or should I say who he thought that I was? I was going to call a cab that night to take me to the nearest Greyhound station until Trap walked up to me and grabbed me close, hugging me as tightly as he could. I'd never felt an embrace so emotional. I could feel his pain through his touch.

"Your mama loves my kids like they're hers," I hesitated to say. "But they're mine, and I will be back for them."

Trap didn't want to hear it. He didn't want to talk about

letting me go, not after the time we'd had moments before his mama's bitch-ass came in, having a temper tantrum.

"You staying?" He buried his face in my neck, ignoring what I'd just said to him.

"Yeah, I'll stay a few more hours," I told him. "I gotta catch a bus to Brielle."

"You're a celebrity wife. You're not taking a fuckin' bus anywhere. I have drivers. One of them can take you where you have to go." Trap let go of me. "This isn't over, Gia." He frowned down at me.

I shook my head in disagreement. "It is, Travis. It was over the day I put that bleach in that baby's bottle. Your mama is right. I'm a mistake."

Trap slid his hands around my neck and into my hair. Gripping my hair a little, he pulled me closer to him. "*My* fuckin' mistake, just like you heard me tell her."

"We're done, Travis." I tried to control my hormones, but his hands around my neck had my pussy throbbing. "Come on now, boy. I still have nut dripping from my asshole."

"'Boy?'" Trap made a face. "I got your 'boy'."

"Do you?" I grinned. "Show me then." I pulled the shirt I was wearing over my head and tossed it on the couch. I barely got the words out when Trap picked me up and carried me to the back, where he fucked me like he wanted his mama to hear my moans from across the hall.

I woke up the next morning sore as fuck. Pushing my hair from my face, I saw Trap packing his things in his suitcase. He grinned at me when he saw me waking up. Before he could say anything, his cell phone rang in his pocket. He was dressed comfortably in black joggers and a plaid purple and black hoodie, perfect attire for a plane ride to wherever they had him going. He took his phone from his pocket, frowning in confusion at the display as if he didn't recognize the number that was calling.

"Shady Medical Center'?" he muttered to himself before answering. "Yo?"

The phone wasn't even on speaker, but I could hear the person on the other end loud and clear. "Nigga, put Gia on the phone."

Trap glared at his phone like he knew the nigga wasn't talking to him. He put the phone back to his ear as he eyed me sitting up in bed.

"Who is that?" I mouthed.

"Yo, who the fuck is this?" Trap snarled.

"Her fuckin' psychiatrist," I heard the deep voice growl back. "Nigga you know who this is. Put my patient on the muthafuckin' phone. I know she's with you. The Baltimore Bayou said they released her. One of your groupies tagged you in a post on IG, saying your wife was back from the nut house. She posted your location, nigga. Paparazzi are surrounding that hotel as we speak, waiting for you to pop out. Control your bitches and protect your wife. And put her on the fuckin' phone."

The whole time the nigga on the other end was talking, Trap was looking at me like he wanted to snap my neck. He didn't hand me the phone. "I don't know who the fuck you think you are, calling my fuckin' phone for *my* fuckin' wife."

"I'm the nigga who kept her warm for you while you were on tour. I hadn't seen her since I saw her walk out of that courthouse the day you two got married. Me and your wife caught up right where we left off at Wake Hills. It was just like old times. Only this time, I got to see how warm she is on the inside."

My eyes widened as I watched Trap's golden skin turn red.

"Knight? Nigga, is this you?" Trap's voice echoed throughout the hotel.

"Muthafucka, it'll always be me." Knight laughed through the phone. "Tell ya wife I'll see her when she gets back in town. Her appointment is at 2:30 tomorrow afternoon."

And the phone hung up.

Gia's ass was crazy for fuckin' with niggas who used to be fuckin' friends. Marrying one and fuckin' the other. Shit, I'd just fucked the shit out of Trap, and by the sound of things, I was gonna fuck the shit out of Knight, too, at my dick appointment the next day at 2:30. If I made it there.

"Shit, nigga, what do you want me to say?" I sat up in bed, eyeing Trap as he glared at me like he was deciding how many pieces he was going to cut Knight into right in front of me.

"Gia, I will cancel this whole fuckin' tour to air Charlotte out. You must not remember me for real." Trap reached for the two Glocks I pretended not to notice on the nightstand. Gia and I were twins—if she liked that gangsta shit, I loved it. "Don't get fucked up."

"Oouuu. I like the sound of that. What I gotta do to get fucked up?" I giggled. I hope the nigga didn't think I was scared. My pussy did a little dance as soon as I saw him tucking those guns into his boxers. The nigga looked good as fuck, by the way. I would've grabbed him and given him a little quickie before he went on tour, but Knight ruined it for me.

"Don't fuckin' play with me, shawty. I will end that nigga's entire family behind you," Trap warned me.

"Nigga, go on tour." I rolled my eyes as I sat on his bed, naked as fuck. "I'm not worried about married-as-fuck Knight Shade. I wasn't in my right mind. I wasn't on my meds. I was hurt, and I blamed you for putting me in that place. It was a phase, and it's over." I eyed the semi-relieved look on Trap's face, and I had to remind him that shit didn't mean things were all good between the two of us either. "You're not off the hook either, Travis. A year is a long time without a husband, let alone without a husband, and in a mental institution. Yeah, I told you not to bring your light-skinned ass up in there, but that didn't mean *not* to bring your light-skinned ass up in there!" I got up from the bed and stood before him.

Trap's temples trembled, and his eyes squinted to get a really good look at me as I shoved him in his chest. "I did my wrong. I did my dirt, and apparently, you did some, too. I hope you don't think you're about to leave me for that nigga."

"I hope you don't think you're about to tell me what the fuck to do after all this time." I scoffed.

Trap laughed. "Okay, Geor'Gia Starr, play with it if you want to." He turned around and walked back over to his luggage. "Wash ya ass and meet me in the lobby."

Knight wasn't lying. Paparazzi were everywhere on the ground floor of that hotel. Trap was still upset with me. It must've sucked to think he stole his homeboy's girl, only for his homeboy to steal her right back. Yet and still, he made sure I got out of there safely. He put me in a separate car to get away from the hotel. His driver was supposed to take me shopping for whatever I needed to drive me all the way from Baltimore back to Charlotte, North Carolina.

However, when we made it to Raleigh, North Carolina, I overheard a customer at a Shell gas station talking about a Champagne Campaign. Every election year, hotels would host parties for politicians running for government offices. I remember that shit like it was yesterday. The Camerons and the LePonts were often invited to those political parties, putting me on display like a piece of sexual meat. As a young girl, I dreaded the occasion. But as Gia Starr, I was going to make a loud-ass entrance in hopes of running into Matthew Tiller, our fucked-up father.

The driver, a Dominican woman who barely spoke English named Carmen, was directed to stay with me until I made it to Charlotte. In other words, Trap wanted her to take me to Charlotte to make sure I wasn't going to that dick appointment with Knight at 2:30. The party was at 6:00 that night, and it was 3:30. I needed to go shopping for a damn dress and maybe some jewelry. I hadn't gone shopping in nine fuckin' years. All those people swarming around me at that mall was overwhelming. And Carmen stood at my side like a damn bodyguard from the Cartel. Driver my ass. I knew a damn killer when I saw one.

After buying a black fitted off-the-shoulder dress and a pair of black Red Bottoms from Saks at Triangle Town Center, I wanted to buy some jewelry from Swavarski at Crabtree Mall. Carmen didn't crack any facial expressions. She stood a few feet behind me, wearing a dark blue dress suit. Her long, sleek hair was pulled back into a ponytail. She looked straight ahead, waiting for some shit to pop off.

"I know this is boring, Carmen." I glanced back at her over my shoulder before looking back at the luxurious jewelry behind the glass. "It's just that I miss diamonds. My family was full of monsters, but they laced me with the finest jewelry, and I miss that sometimes. My family used to abuse me in every way imaginable, but I miss the diamonds." I laughed to myself. "Is that crazy?"

"No," Carmen answered after not saying shit to me for almost seven hours. "Los diamantes son los mejores amigos de una chica."

"The fuck does that mean?" My face scrunched in confusion.

"Diamonds are a girl's best friend," Carmen responded.

Before I could answer, one of the white women who worked there approached me. The bitch had been watching me for fifteen fuckin' minutes. She acted like I was casing the place before I robbed the muthafucka.

She faked a smile as I looked up at her in frustration.

Before she could be fake enough to ask if I needed help with anything, I snapped, "Bitch, I will cut you."

She held up her hands defensively before walking away, muttering to herself, "If you need anything, let one of us know."

I rolled my eyes, looking back down at the beautiful diamond bracelet and matching earrings.

"Moms has that set," a deep male voice chimed in. "I think I'm gonna get her the matching necklace. Maybe a watch, too."

I looked to my left at this chocolate muthafucka with the cutest dimples piercing his cheeks, even though he wasn't even smiling. I wasn't sure why I got a familiar feeling when I was in his presence, but I did. I brushed it off, already annoyed at Becky thinking I was gonna rob the place.

"Going on a date or something, mamas?" he asked, turning to me in his suit and tie, looking like one of those rich black niggas who thought they were better than everyone who wasn't in their position.

"No, not that. I'm married." I flashed my ring at him, which he didn't even bother to look at. "I'm going to a Champagne Campaign."

His eyebrows rose a little. "Oh, word? At the Embassy Suites? Yeah, I got invited to that. Just here buying some jewelry for moms to wear to this bullshit, too. Thinking about getting this emerald watch over here to go with her evening gown. What are you wearing? Are you going alone? I know everyone on that list who's going, and I didn't see your name."

"Nigga, it's because my name ain't on the list. I see you

know my name is Gia Starr, which means you know who my man is." I rolled my eyes as I faced him.

He frowned a little, shaking his head at me. "Your name isn't no fuckin' Gia Starr. You look more like a London. London with a 'y'."

My heart jumped in my chest as he grabbed my left forearm, turning it so he could see the scar that ran from my wrist to my elbow. I looked back into his face.

"Where did you get this scar?" he asked as I yanked away from him.

I hesitated, looking into his face. "What's it to you?"

Chocolate laughed a little. "I knew this girl once when I went to school for about a year or two in Glen Burnie, up in Maryland. She was a tiny little thing. She was in gymnastics. She used to flip off everything in the playground. You remind me of her."

I shook my head, heart trembling in my chest. "I-I never went to school in Maryland."

"I met her in sixth grade," he went on to explain, despite my denial. "I met her the day she flipped off the monkey bars and broke her arm. The bone went straight through her skin. All the kids were screaming for help. I walked over calmly, kneeled down beside her, and popped it back in place. And I held it until the ambulance came."

I turned my arm, looking at the scar, remembering the boy from that day. I looked back into his face. He *did* look familiar. I remembered those dimples and the silky texture of his tightly curled hair. That little boy applied pressure to my arm, blood gushing between his fingers. He was just as calm as could be. I'll never forget him singing to me. He sang Wanya's famous verse from "Bended Knee" to my soul that day. That little muthafucka said he wanted a new life, and he wanted that shit with me. An eleven-year-old boy singing from his heart. Hell yeah, I remembered that shit, but I wasn't about to admit that shit to his cocky ass.

"Hell nah, I don't remember you, nigga." I played it off, trying my best not to stutter. "What-what did you say your name was?" I never got his name that day.

"I didn't. My name back when we were in school was Winter Shade." The man watched me, still looking at him in denial with a hint of curiosity.

"*Was?*" I hesitated to ask what he meant by that.

"My mama changed my name because she didn't want me to be affiliated with that name. When my stepfather adopted me, my name was changed. I'm Rigel. Rigel Worth." Rigel held out his hand to shake mine. "Now, don't tell me your name is Gia Starr when I know for a fact it's not. You might look like her, but anyone who really knows her will know you're not her even though you're wearing scrubs from the Baltimore Bayou."

I gasped a little, looking back over my shoulder at Carmen, who was already looking my way. When she started to approach, I shook my head at her before looking back into Rigel's face. "What the fuck do you want?" I muttered through my teeth.

"Nothing. Yet." Rigel chuckled a little. "Twins, huh? Oh, I'm a lawyer, by the way. Some hire me as a private investigator. I can find out anything on anyone." He grinned at the shook expression on my face.

"Trap." I exhaled deeply, realizing the nigga was following me. Realizing *Trap* had the nigga following me, or should I say Gia. "*You're* how he found Gia."

My heart felt like it was about to explode. If he knew everything about Gia, he had to know about me. He had to know that I wasn't supposed to be free. That I was the one who'd committed the crimes that she'd originally been accused of. I looked at him as he continued to look at the jewelry.

"I did it to save her life," I told him. "Our own father was fuckin' her!"

Rigel nodded. "I know."

"Are you gonna turn me in?" I asked.

Rigel shook his head. "Nah. You did what you had to do."

I hesitated, watching him signal Becky to come over. "What is it that you want from me, nigga?" I asked again.

"Like I said, nothing *yet*," he repeated himself. He faked a smile once Becky stood before him on the other side of the jewelry counter. "Yeah, I want that watch right there and that necklace right there. I'd like them wrapped up, please. Oh, and whatever Mrs. Gia Starr right here wants as well."

"I'm still looking." I smacked my lips at the bitch as she walked away to grab some gift boxes for the jewelry that she was about to get for Rigel out of the case. I looked back at Rigel, watching him look me over. "I don't need shit from you."

"Oh, I know, Mrs. LePont. Your mother-in-law left a fortune for her murderer. I would've hung the bitch, too, if she treated me like a house nigga." Rigel scoffed. "What jewelry are you wearing on our date tonight?"

"Who said I was going anywhere with you?" I huffed.

"You can't get in without an invite. My stepfather is hosting this event," Rigel let me know. "So, again, I'm asking, what jewelry are you going to wear tonight?"

I kinda liked the muthafucka, even though I wasn't sure if I could trust him.

It took everything in me not to call Jaliyah and ask her to let Gia call me. Or, should I say, ask her to let Londyn call *me* since I was supposed to be Gia. I needed to know more about Rigel. About who he was. Gia mentioned that Marley was playing get back because Gia was fuckin' her nigga, Knight, but Trap had an entire private investigator trailing Gia. An investigator who knew the entire time that Gia had a twin sister. Who knew the entire time that *I* was her twin sister who was locked up for fuckin' murder and was supposed to die at that mental institution. And why the fuck did his mama change his fuckin' name? He needed me for something.

Rigel went so far as to reserve a room for me in his name so no one would know Gia Starr was staying at the hotel. Not just that, but he had Carmen take me to the beauty supply store for a short wig and dark shades. I told Carmen that I was good and she could head on back to Maryland. Rigel promised to get me to Charlotte safely and away from Knight. That was all she needed to hear to go on her way. I didn't want her to get caught up in my shit.

I wanted to cause a scene, but Rigel wanted me to lay low. And I agreed until I saw my father over the punch table. He was on his third drink when I was about to get up from the table and go over to pay my disrespects.

"Gia Starr," Rigel called out to me just as I stood from my seat.

I huffed, turning toward him as he walked up to me with a short, attractive woman who looked like the pretty female version of him.

"Mama, this is Gia Starr. Gia, this is my mother, Agnes Worth," Rigel introduced.

His mother glared at me a little, muttering something to her son in another language before faking a smile. "You remind me of the white woman he used to date. What's this one's story, eh?"

I'd had enough of niggas and their mothers for one day. "Oh, you don't want to know my story. Your story, on the other hand, might end right here if you don't get the fuck out of my face."

Agnes laughed mischievously. "The many ways I could kill you without even touching you."

I frowned, about to snatch that bitch by her fuckin' lips, when Rigel shoved his mother in the opposite direction and stood in my path, so I couldn't snatch the bitch by her braids. "Other white woman, Rigel?" I shoved him. "Did the bitch just slick call me white?"

"She doesn't like light skins." Rigel laughed a little. "I knew she'd distract you from doing something fuckin' stupid." His smile quickly faded. "Matthew has plenty of backup in this bitch. He may look like he's alone, but trust me, the muthafucka is definitely *not* alone. Every cook, bartender, janitor, or what your family considers the help works for that nigga. As soon as it looks like you're about to say the wrong thing to him, they will shoot you in the head and keep on partying."

"Not master being a thug." I huffed, looking around the room at all the rich white folks, a few of my foster family and ex-husband's family included.

Honestly, I blended in pretty well with everyone. The wig was actually pretty cute, and the makeup he had me cake on my face actually made me unrecognizable. The last time any of my family had seen me, I was on the stand, looking like a mix between Samara and Beloved. They hadn't seen me cleaned up nicely in nine years. And all those honey buns and psych meds had me super thick those days. I saw the way Rigel didn't even try to hide the fact that he couldn't keep his eyes off my hips and thighs. I wanted to trust him based on those handsome chocolate features of his alone, but the fact that a lawyer knew I was supposed to be sitting in a psych ward for multiple murders and hadn't turned me in wasn't sitting well with me.

"You smell nice." He leaned over to get a quick whiff of my neck. "What's that fragrance? Serial killer and rose petals?"

I rolled my eyes over to him, glaring as he took a sip of whatever he was drinking from his glass. "Nah, it's 'kiss my ass, nigga' with a hint of 'the fuck do you want from me?' Smells good, don't it?"

"Intoxicating." Rigel chuckled, looking over my shoulder toward the entrance. His eyebrows lowered into a tight frown.

I looked over my shoulder in the direction he was looking. I'd never seen the Shade family in person, only on commercials or talk shows about their medical system. I'd recognize Knight Shade anywhere. Jaliyah was obsessed with the family's clinical trials and would make me try whatever psych medicine the family would administer to their patients. If Knight gave his patients crack cocaine laced with Gorilla Glue and pink glitter, best believe she would give me that shit. Then I thought for a minute before looking at Rigel's angry expression.

"Wait a minute—at the jewelry counter, you told me that your name used to be Winter Shade. Nigga, are those your people?" My eyes widened.

"Nah, the Worths are my people." Rigel smiled, removing his glare from Knight walking in the door and putting it on my face. "Go over to the punch table and ask Mr. Tiller where the Coke is."

I frowned in confusion. "Muthafucka, ask him where the *Coke* is?"

"You know your people snort that shit. Ask him where it is and go with him to get it." Rigel shoved me forward a little.

I smoothed out my dress as I headed toward the punch table. I'd never stood face-to-face with my biological father. I'd only learned he was my father a few years ago. The closest view I'd gotten of him was watching him leave the Bayou the night he raped my sister. Walking up to the table, I wanted to crack the punch bowl over his head, but it was obvious that Rigel had some sort of plan. Though I wanted to kill the muthafucka in broad daylight, I kept my crazy contained for the moment. Gia needed me to clear things up with our big sister before switching places. Well, she wanted me to let her rot in my room, but I definitely intended to go back to life at the psych ward as soon as I played outside for a little while.

Matthew eyed me over the rim of his glass as I poured myself a glass of whatever semi-sweet punch them folks made. If it weren't for the alcohol in that punch, I would've spit the shit out. The shit was barely sweet. There must've been one piece of sugar in that nasty shit.

"The fuck kind of punch is this?" I made a face as I took a little sip.

"My wife, Jessie, made the punch. You don't like it?" Matthew laughed a little.

The white nigga was actually good-looking. Looked something like an older Keanu Reeves. No wonder I never liked *The Matrix*. He stood there, dark black curly hair falling to his shoulders. Navy blue Armani suit. Patent leather Armani shoes. Vintage Rolex on his wrist. He was definitely high as fuck and looked like he hadn't slept in days.

"You're Matthew Tiller?" I turned to him. "You're running for senator this year."

"Did you vote?" He faced me, looking me over a little. He looked back into my face, his eyebrows rising a little as if it dawned on him who I was.

"For you? Hell no." I laughed a little, about to take a sip from my drink, forgetting how nasty the shit was. I set the cup on the table. "I have my money on one of the LePonts. Kennedy is in office now; I'm sure Denny will win the seat. You definitely don't deserve to be in office. I hear you like little girls, close relatives, to be specific."

"Do I know you?" he asked.

"Do you want to?" I grinned a little, moving in closer. "I need whatever you're on right now. I need some shit that'll have me floating. Can you hook me up? I'm gonna need something if I have to sit through this boring shit."

Matthew nodded. "Are you staying in the building?"

I hesitated but nodded in agreement. "Yes, I am. Room 420."

"I hope you don't mind. I bought some friends." Matthew grinned, walking past me and into my hotel room about twenty minutes after I gave him the invitation.

I exhaled deeply, eying three tall black men walking into the room behind him. I closed the door behind them and watched the three men stand a few feet behind Matthew as he sat on the sofa and rolled up his sleeves.

I slowly approached him, watching as he took out a few tiny bags of coke from his pocket and carefully made a few lines on the glass coffee table.

"You can take off that wig, Gia," Matthew snarled, getting straight to the point. "I heard you were released yesterday. Congratulations."

I knew it was too easy getting the muthafucka to come to my room. I was sure he thought I was scared of him, but I'd definitely been around way worse than him. He'd fucked my twin's head up so much that she split into three different bitches. Just one of me was crazy enough to face him. I grew up with nothing but foster brothers, foster uncles, and perverted male foster cousins. Sofia was speaking for me when she said all her life she had to fight. She wasn't lying when she said a woman ain't safe in a family of men. If Matthew thought I was afraid, he was sadly mistaken.

"And wipe off that make-up from your face. You don't need that shit." The muthafucka glared up at me before taking more bags of cocaine from his pocket and placing them on the glass table. He removed his blazer and draped it across the chair behind him. "Come sit next to Daddy. Let's talk about my family members that your sister killed for you." He grinned as I sat next to him, removing my wig from my head and tossing it onto the table.

I removed the stocking cap and threw it over with the wig.

The pervert eyed my curly hair, falling to my shoulders. He exhaled deeply like he was reminiscing about the times he'd forced himself inside me. "You smell nice. You never smell this nice. You smell rich instead of like psych meds. What's the occasion?"

"You said you wanted to know why my sister shot the security guards and stomped holes in the nurses. She would've popped one of the nurses' heads from her body like a cork if a few of the patients she'd freed from their rooms hadn't pulled her off the bitch. She couldn't stand by and watch you get away with raping me. White nigga, we have a fuckin' baby!" I watched my father laugh out loud before rolling a hundred-dollar bill and snorting two of the lines.

Matthew sat up, throwing his head back in ecstasy, probably feeling an instant high. He held his hand up in my direction, letting me know it was my turn. "Your turn."

I barely got the chance to shake my head when that muthafucka grabbed me by the neck and forced my head down to the coffee table. As soon as he let go of my neck, I gasped for air, inhaling the powder that he'd smushed my face into. When I came up for air, I smacked that nigga dead in his face. I didn't realize the muthafucka was already prepared for me to fight back. I barely stung his peach skin when he cut me from my wrist to my elbow with the pocketknife he had in his hand. He'd reopened my old wound. I dropped to my knees between the sofa and the coffee table.

Matthew laughed to himself as he stood before me, rolling up the sleeves of his silk dress shirt. "I see you forgot who the fuck is in charge here." He grabbed me up from the floor by my hair.

I didn't dare let out a sound as I grimaced in pain. I held my bleeding arm in my hands, looking him in the face as he started to unzip his pants. "Do it. Muthafucka, I dare you!" I cringed in pain as he grabbed my hair from the roots.

His men stood around, watching him about to assault his own fuckin' daughter.

Just when he started to pull his meat out, the door to the room in the back opened.

"Gonna swallow my pride, say I'm sorry. Stop pointing fingers. The blame is on me." The heavy metal sound of a barrel cocking echoed through the hallway.

Matthew let go of my hair and turned to face the music.

Oh, yeah, Rigel was in the back, waiting for me to say the magic words, "Do it, muthafucka."

The security guards barely got the chance to reach for their weapons before Rigel was already firing at the muthafuckas. He shot and killed two of them, shooting both in the head. He shot the third one in the arm, who was reaching for the gun, and then he shot the muthafucka's right leg. Before Matthew could run toward the security guard's weapon that had dropped to the ground, Rigel shot his ass twice in his neck.

"I want a new life, and I want it with you. If you feel the same, don't ever let it go." Rigel continued to sing as he walked over the dead bodies toward the six-foot-five muthafucka who'd fallen to the floor in pain. He snatched the muthafucka up by his locs. "You were really gonna let this nigga make his own daughter suck his pink dick? The only reason you're not fuckin' dead is because you're gonna tell the police I killed these niggas to protect her from him. Do you fuckin' hear me?" Rigel dug his gun into the man's jaw. "Nigga, I said, *do you fuckin' hear me?*"

"Yeah, yeah, nigga, I got it!" the man screamed in pain.

"I know that muthafucka was paying you well enough to get your fuckin' hair twisted. Lookin' like Lil' Wayne and shit, three-dreadlocks-having ass." Rigel tossed the nigga's head to the left before walking over to help me off the floor. He looked remorsefully into my face as he carefully sat me on the couch. "We had to let him get close enough to put his hands on you to claim self-defense. I'm sorry he cut you, but you needed to get rid of that scar if you're claiming to be Gia."

"How could someone's father treat them like this?" I looked up into his face, blood gushing from my wound. I felt the effects of that coke sinking into my soul. I didn't even feel the pain in my arm, just the wetness from the blood seeping through my fingers and dripping onto my dress.

Rigel's thick eyebrows connected tightly. "I don't know, but he's gone now."

I looked over at Matthew lying on the floor, my heart running at full speed in my chest. I eyed the security guard, trying to reach for his gun. Before I could let Rigel know the muthafucka was reaching for his gun on the floor, Rigel rose from the couch and shot the stupid muthafucka in his hand.

The security guard cried out in pain.

"Lil Wayne, do you want to fuckin' live long enough to make it to the fuckin' hospital?" Rigel walked toward him, picking up the man's gun and aiming the gun at his head. "Reach for your fuckin' phone and call 911!"

Just as the security guard cried out in pain, about to reach for his phone in his pocket, there was a knock at the door.

"Room service." A woman's voice seeped through the heavy door.

Rigel aimed both guns at the door. "If it's room service, use your card and come in."

The door clicked open, and in came a pretty dark-skinned woman dressed in scrubs from the hospital. She stepped inside, hand behind her back, eyeing Rigel's arms extended, gun aiming at her.

"Slowly put your gun down on the floor and tell your fuckin' brother to come in this muthafucka. I know he's with you, Sable," Rigel snarled at the pretty lady.

Knight stepped into the room, gun in hand, but it was at his side. He saw me on the sofa, holding my arm, blood oozing from my wound between my fingers. He looked over at my father, who was bleeding out on the floor, and one of my father's guards, wounded but still very much alive.

Before Knight could speak, Rigel yelled, "Are you gonna worry about what the fuck I'm doing here, or are one of you muthafuckas gonna call the fuckin' police?"

CHAPTER FOUR
RIGEL

"Tell us again what happened." Officer Lani Daith sat across from me in the waiting room at WakeMed Hospital. She was with five other officers who were waiting to hear my story.

I knew all of them. All of them were children of someone in my stepfather's circle. I've known every officer in that waiting room since I was in elementary school. I knew what I was doing when I killed those muthafuckas in Londyn's hotel room.

"I told you a million fuckin' times," I huffed. "I was asleep in the back when I heard Gia's father come into her room and attack her. Those men were watching that man try to sexually assault her! When I came out of the room, two of them came down the hallway, guns drawn, about to shoot me! I pulled out my gun and shot first. Then the third security guard tried to get to his gun when I shot him enough to wound him so he could corroborate my fuckin' story."

"Senator Tiller was accused of having a baby with Gia, his own daughter. It was never proven but was brought up in court according to gossip on social media," Officer Freddy Myers chimed in. "Did he really have a daughter with his *own* daughter?"

"I don't know, Freddy. Why don't we wake the muthafucka from death and ask him?" I snarled at the idiot. "And he wasn't a fuckin' senator *yet*. Tell his family I'm sorry for his bitch-ass loss."

"His family is very powerful." Lani huffed. "Self-defense or protecting this girl from harm isn't enough to protect you from that family. You put your stepfather's entire law firm at risk—you know that's what Mr. Clark Worth is going to say."

I exhaled deeply, leaning back in my seat.

"You know the Shade family is accusing you of poisoning Brielle Timing." Lani watched me make a face.

"I don't know what the fuck you're talking about," I told the bitch. I never did like Lani. She always liked adding more fuel to the fire. "Who's accusing me of poisoning Brielle?"

"She had a miscarriage a few days ago. The hospital found a large amount of misoprostol in her system. The only thing that's saving you right now is the fact that the autopsy report proves the baby was dead for days before she miscarried," Lani explained. "That girl had a complete hysterectomy after they found a tumor in her uterus. You might want to leave before the Shade family comes back. Everyone knows Knight is involved with Gia. Shit, his own wife knows. Go home. We'll call you if we have any more questions. And you know there *will* be more questions."

"Fuck your questions. *I* have questions!" I frowned. "Where are you getting this information about Brielle? I didn't poison her. The fuck is misoprostol?"

"Son, what happened?" I heard my mother's voice behind me.

I rose from my seat, turning to face her. A concerned look

covered her face as she came around the chairs to confront the officers standing before me. Though you may think I helped kill Brielle's baby, I didn't. I knew Brielle hated my mother showing up in the morning doing the things that I wished Brielle would do around the house. I just wanted Brielle to eat the food that Marley made. I knew it pissed her off the night before to see me dancing with Marley, and I just wanted her to feel the pain I felt when I found out she was fuckin' Shadow.

Truth be told, Marley was keeping an eye on Brielle's prenatal visits for me. That night, when she called me up to tell me where to find Gia, she also told me that there had been no fetal movement for days. I told my mother to make the tea to speed up the process of Brielle expelling the baby. My mother is a midwife. She knew they'd make Brielle push that dead baby out. She did the shit as a favor to me. I played stupid, but I knew helping induce that miscarriage would bring the Shades straight to me, where I wanted them.

Mama walked up and hugged me tightly before releasing me. "What is going on? They say you killed that politician and his security guards! For that white woman?"

I ignored my mother's statement about Londyn's complexion. Mama always hated lighter-skinned women because those were normally the type of women she'd catch my biological father with. She claimed the apple didn't fall too far from the twisted tree. I liked all flavors, but the ones who gravitated toward me were normally the red ones. Mama always said they were referred to as red because they were demons. Maybe some, but definitely not Londyn.

I'd had a fetish for that girl since the day I pushed her bone back through her broken skin. She was the real reason I decided to take private investigator work on the side in the first place. I was trying to find her—fuck Gia. Fuck the shit Brielle was doing behind my back. Though the SAFE program helped thousands of women get away from their abusers, fuck that shit, too, honestly. Shadow's only motive for helping fund Brielle's program was to get her in his bed. And my initial motive for getting involved with Brielle was to find her sister, Londyn.

I knew about Gia's escape from that mental institution before Trap did. I sent out a spam advertisement to the nigga's email, advertising my law firm. I knew helping him find Gia would lead me straight to Londyn. Guess the apple didn't fall too far from the twisted tree at all, huh?

"We'll be in touch." Lani rolled her eyes a little as she was a light skinned chick herself. The rest of the police officers followed her out of the lobby.

I knew I'd be seeing them soon. Like she said, I killed a politician. I'd need to surround myself with hittas 24/7, if nothing else. I had a crew in almost every establishment I visited, as well as in nearly every neighborhood in Charlotte and surrounding areas. Not to mention in Raleigh surrounding that hospital. I had enemies far and wide because I'd often defend notorious drug dealers. Their enemies were always watching me, and I had niggas watching them.

I watched them leave before observing Mama as she pulled a compact mirror out of her purse to make sure her makeup was flawless. "Ma, you got these muthafuckas thinking I poisoned ol' girl."

Mama rolled her eyes. "Frankie's mother made a tea to induce cramping like I asked her to do. Frankie didn't know the girl's baby was already dead. She had her mother make the shit strong to make sure the little bastard was *dead* dead. The nurse staff said they could hear Brielle screaming from the ambulance." Mama chuckled a little. "Oh, come on, it's funny. She got what she deserved. She didn't need to have any more of that devil's children. Frankie had enough for them both."

I didn't want to talk about Brielle. I needed to talk to Londyn and see if she was okay. I knew she was losing her mind, worrying about Gia back at The Bayou. I wanted to ask her how she managed to trade places with her sister, but I knew she wouldn't trust me enough to give me that information. I was just glad to have her around. Her presence was intoxicating.

"Marley called your office looking for you." Mama shoved me a little.

I frowned a little, about to ask her what Marley wanted, when I looked over her shoulder and saw Knight entering the waiting room with his brother Shadow. I grinned because it was the moment I'd been waiting for since I was six. I knew who Shadow was when I agreed to take my colleague's place that day as his lawyer, but it was obvious he didn't realize who I was until he saw me standing in that hospital lobby with my mother.

Mama saw the look on my face as Knight and Shadow made their way over to us in that empty area of the waiting room. Despite how quiet the hospital was that night, my mama knew how much noise the three of us would make if I confronted the brothers the way I wanted to. I was fuckin' the wife of one and had just broken up with the no-baby mama of the other. Shadow knew Brielle and I were together, and he was fuckin' her anyway. I defended his child support case, telling the court all that shit Brielle told me about her own best friend to make her *lose* that best friend. Frankie had her fucked-up ways, but she loved Brielle. Looked up to her even though she hated on her a little. Frankie loved Shadow, too, and she deserved to know her baby's father was fuckin' on her best friend.

"Rigel, this is not the place," Mama tried to tell me before I moved her out of the way to confront the muthafuckas.

"Nah, looks like these two niggas have something they want to say to me." I chuckled.

Mama got back in front of me when Shadow got in her face.

"Bitch, you might want to move," Shadow snarled down at my mama, who was barely five feet tall.

"Nigga, you really wanna do this here?" I showed them the gun I had tucked in my dress pants.

Both niggas did the same. I guess all three of us avoided getting frisked at the metal detectors that night.

"Shit, we can," Knight let me know. "You've been fuckin' my wife, nigga, then your mama here tried to kill Brielle's baby out of spite for your girl sneakin' with my brother!"

"That white woman's baby was already dead when I helped induce her labor! And you know who told me that? *Your* wife," Mama snapped.

Knight wasn't sure what to say at that moment, but I was.

"You don't remember me, do you, Knight? Nah, you don't." I watched confusion take over his face. "But *you* do." I turned to Shadow. "Until two years ago, I hadn't seen you since I was six. I watched you put a gun to my mama's head and fuck her in front of the nigga she was cheating on you with. After you made that man watch you have sex with her, you shot him in front of her. You pulled your pants up and walked past me while I was standing in the door watching."

Shadow's temples twitched as he watched me dig into my pockets. He wasn't sure what I was reaching for, so he reached for his gun, pulling it out of his pants.

I pulled out the gold engraved pocket watch that I always kept with me. "You gave me this watch when I was three years old, remember? You had my name, Winter Shade, engraved on the back. Remember, Pops?"

"Pops? The fuck is he talking about, Shadow?" Knight howled in confusion.

"I held onto this piece of shit because it was the only piece of you I had when you left me, nigga." I shoved the watch into Shadow's chest. "*She* cheated on you, muthafucka. It wasn't me! You didn't have to leave me! I didn't have shit to do with that!"

Shadow's dark skin turned red with anger. He didn't say shit. He just looked at me with the same look in his eyes as he had the day he saw my mama fuckin' another nigga in his bed. At first, he didn't even get angry when he saw her fuckin' that man. I watched him get naked and climb into bed with them. The nigga got up and out of the way, about to reach for his gun, when Shadow beat him to it. He shot the nigga in his shoulder before aiming the gun at Mama's head. He told her he wanted some pussy, too, since she was just giving the shit away like candy. He cocked the barrel back, and she screamed for him not to kill her. Mama was never the same after that day, and neither was I.

"Knight was there that day. He was in the living room, playing video games. The very next day, your mother was killed, huh?" I laughed a little, remembering the fact that Mama was the one who contacted my crazy preaching grandfather to let him know where his ex-wife was eating breakfast the next morning. I was sure Shadow had always wondered how his father found their mother that day.

Knight really wanted to blow my head off, but his brother stood in his way. "Shadow, are you listening to this shit?" He shoved his brother aside to hear me talk some more of my bullshit.

"Nigga, are *you* hearing this shit?" I laughed, sitting back in my chair and leaning back comfortably, wishing the nigga would bust a move so I could blow his jaw off. "While you're over here playing doctor with Gia, your wife is sitting at home waiting for you. Well, she *was* sitting home waiting for you until you got sloppy. Trap hired me to find Gia. I knew she was in Charlotte the entire time; I just didn't know exactly where she'd been hiding. That was until your wife told me if I was looking for Gia, I could find her underneath you, nigga. How long did you think you could continue to fuck another nigga's wife before another nigga started fuckin' yours?"

Shadow had to use all the strength he had to pull Knight away from me. "Yo, chill!"

Knight pulled away, pushing his brother off him. "Nigga, *you* chill! This nigga is *your* problem! You handle him before I do!" Knight snarled before he spotted a doctor who came out of the double doors, waiting for one of us to approach him to get the news about Gia. Knight glared at me before going over to the doctor.

Shadow's eyes followed his brother. As soon as he saw his brother sighing in relief at the news the doctors had given him, he sat in the chair across from me. He glanced at Mama as she sat alongside me. I was sure he had questions for her, wondering if she was really ruthless enough to have his mother killed because he'd killed her side nigga. But he let it go for the time being.

"I don't know what you're doing here with Gia Starr, but you need to back the fuck off," Shadow called himself warning me.

"Or else what?" I scoffed. "Trap is paying me to watch his girl until he comes back from tour. He told me to keep her the fuck away from The Shades."

"Too bad he doesn't know you *are* one." Shadow huffed, clutching the watch I'd given back to him in his hands.

"Nigga, I'm a Worth," I reminded him. "You made sure of that."

Shadow laughed a little, shaking his head at the situation. "You defended me in court against Frankie. You got me full custody of my kids. You humiliated Brielle in court so you could win. The entire time, you knew I was your father?"

"Did you know the entire time that you were fuckin' Brielle that she was my girlfriend?" My voice echoed throughout the waiting room. "Did you ever once stop to think that what you were doing was fucked up?"

"You're fuckin' around with Knight's wife—your *uncle's* wife—because of me?" Shadow had the balls to ask.

I sat up in my chair. "Nigga, I fucked the doctor's wife because he was fuckin' Gia, my client's wife."

"You didn't have to involve Marley in this. She has enough issues," Shadow reminded me.

"Who wouldn't, fuckin' with this family?" I couldn't help but laugh. "Muthafucka, until I traded places with my cousin, Royce, as your attorney, I hadn't stood face to face with you since I was fuckin' six years old. Nigga, *six!*" I stood from the chair.

Mama tried to grab my arm, but I pulled away as Shadow stood from his seat.

I approached Shadow, yelling in his face, wishing he'd reach for his gun again so I could blow his brains out in that hospital. "You left me and never looked the fuck back! Another man raised your son, and he did a better job at it than you ever could! How do you feel about that shit?"

Shadow finally cracked a smile after looking like a fuckin' statue the entire time. "You made it without me. I knew your mother was the one who pointed my father in the direction to find my mother. I spared her because killing her would start a war between the Shades and the Fall family. I wasn't ready for war then, but I'm ready now. Stay the fuck away from Brielle.

Stay the fuck away from Gia. And stay the *fuck* away from my sister-in-law. You got that? Everything you are, everything you'll ever be is because the *Shade* blood runs through your fuckin' veins, nigga. You remember that shit. You just killed a white politician and his goons and injured one who will probably die today from his wounds. You've got more problems than me. Talk some sense into your son, Agnes." Shadow winked at Mama before looking at me. He chuckled a little before turning to walk away. "Appreciate the help in court, Rigel Worth, Esquire."

"Brielle's nigga, huh?" Londyn huffed at me as I pulled up a chair at her bedside that night in the hospital. "*You're* Brielle's boyfriend? Knight and Marley were Gia's friends from that group home–*that* much, she told me. She also said that Marley was fuckin' Brielle's man to possibly get back at her for fuckin' Knight. Gia said that Marley purposely exposed Gia being in that SAFE program to fuck up Brielle's shit. Gia thinks Brielle hates her! Is the program ruined? Has it really been exposed to the public?"

I hesitated to answer. "No one has exposed the whereabouts of the survivors of the program or who runs it. The police prematurely gave the press a statement about Gia using 'some sort of domestic violence program' to escape The Bayou. Brielle's secret is still safe."

"She's still in the hospital, you know. She gets out in a few days. Maybe I'll get to talk to her before my dick appointment with Knight Shade at 2:30." Londyn rolled her misty eyes. "Has Trap called?"

I nodded, eying her trembling hand. "Yeah. Nigga was just about to walk on stage, and he called to see if you made it to

Charlotte safely. He hadn't seen the news, and I didn't feel the need to tell him."

"Politicians are ruthless, Winter." Londyn sank back into her pillows.

I looked at her. "Don't call me that shit."

"You like pretending to be something you're not? Because I don't." Londyn wiped the tear that fell from her eye. "I wanted to be the one to kill that muthafucka. I was supposed to do to him what he did to my sister."

"Well, it was time for the devil to collect." I watched the tears continue to fall from her eyes. "Hopefully, Satan is doing to the sick politician what he did to your sister. You let me worry about that."

Londyn shook her head. "You're not in this alone. Brielle is going to hate me for this, but you're not in this alone. Since Brielle won't be out of the hospital for a few days, can I stay with you?"

I looked at her, not really sure how to respond. My uncle was in love with who he thought she was. Stay with me? Hell fuckin' yeah. "Y-yeah, that's cool. I have space." I wasn't expecting shawty to want to stay with a nigga after finding out I wasn't just a nigga who helped her on the playground but her sister's ex.

Londyn nodded, drying her face even though the tears continued. "So... my big sister is hunchin' on your daddy, huh? Fucked up. Did you love my sister?"

"We were supposed to be in love, but... I don't even think I really know how to do that shit. She did, but not with me. She didn't want a nigga until I was fuckin' another nigga's wife." I couldn't keep watching her cry. I reached for her warm face and dried her tears.

She covered my hand with hers for a second, embracing the

moment before moving my hands from her face. "Do you love Marley? Your uncle's wife, Marley?"

"Picture me having feelings for someone who's still chasing a nigga who's in love with someone else. Someone who's in love with you," I reminded her.

Londyn shook her head. "Knight doesn't love Gia. He doesn't even realize that I'm not her. Trap didn't realize it, either. You took one look at me and knew I wasn't Gia, and you haven't seen me since we were eleven. What is that telling you?" She laughed, holding her bandaged arm.

"I see your scars, that's all," I told her.

Londyn grinned a little. "Knight gave me Brielle's phone number. I'm scared to call her. I haven't seen her since I was two, but I still remember her face. I know I don't deserve to be free, but I'm glad I am, even if it's just for a little while."

I frowned a little. "A little while?"

"I'm just trying to help my sister get things right, then I'm going back to The Bayou." Londyn peeped the disappointed yet irritated expression on my face. "You're a lawyer. You're supposed to abide by the law. You know they need to lock me up and throw away the key."

"How many law-abiding lawyers do you know?" I scoffed. "Muthafuckas find loopholes and ways to bend the justice system every day. I've seen people get off for way more heinous crimes than what you committed. I'm gonna figure out a way to free my nigga."

Londyn grinned a little, looking as though she liked the sound of that. "Thanks for noticing my scars. I'd thought you'd be the devil the way Gia described what she knew about you. She never said your name, but I was sure it was Satan T. Devil."

"Yeah? Well, even that nigga has a story. Ya married nigga's brother told me to stay away from you, and the man who thinks he's your husband told me to make sure that married nigga stays away from you. I'm sorry Mama drugged your sister, but the baby was already dead. She wasn't trying to kill her," I lied to myself.

Londyn pursed her lips. "Have you met that African voodoo priestess of a mother you have? I could feel the venom brewing inside her. And where the fuck is this Frankie? I'd love to meet her." She cracked her knuckles. "I'm sure she didn't know the baby was already dead. You used her to stir up trouble, dirty bastard. Why can't you use your evil for good?"

I resented that. "I used that shit for good when that white nigga sliced your arm open, now didn't I? I'm Winter only when I need to be. I'll be him for you, that's it."

There that pretty grin was again. "You spending the night, evil twin? Or do you have someplace you need to be?"

I did have shit to do. I had a shit load of paperwork to clear from my desk, not to mention about three briefs to work on. Marley had been blowing my phone up over the past few days from the moment Gia was put in that straight jacket and thrown into the back of a police car. She was bound to pop up sooner or later. Probably at my office since I wasn't picking up the phone or answering her texts.

"Nah, I'm stayin'," I told her and watched her wink at me.

I had a change of clothes in the gym bag in my trunk. I brought it in so I'd have something to change into and wouldn't have to wear that fuckin' suit in the morning. Shawty had a nigga watching Law and Order SVU all night, and I got on her nerves finding all the errors the district attorney made. She fell asleep after her last dose of pain meds, and I fell asleep in the recliner in the corner of the room.

I woke up the next morning to the sound of the shower running and what sounded like Londyn screaming at someone.

"Ma'am, you're not supposed to be in the shower. You're

supposed to keep your bandages dry. Please don't throw that at me. Ma'am—"

The nurse standing in the doorway of the bathroom ducked as a few bottles of hospital shampoo went flying at her.

"Get the fuck out!" Londyn screamed. "I'm talking to Gia!"

I got up, yawning, as I reached for my gym bag, which was on the floor next to the recliner. I dug through the bag for my hygiene bag and then got up from the chair.

The nurse looked at me, seemingly irritated that I was coming to her rescue too slowly. Shit, she was the dummy for standing there, letting someone throw shit at her. Couldn't pay me to let muthafuckas throw shit at me. "She's Gia, right? Why does she keep saying she's talking to Gia?" The nurse huffed.

I peeped the nurse's name tag before looking into her face. "Did you *ask* her?" I huffed back, approaching the door as she moved out of the way to let me step inside.

There, Londyn sat on the floor of the tile shower, legs bent at the knees, arms wrapped around her legs. "She's in trouble. Gia's in trouble. I can feel her. I can always feel her. The last time I ignored these feelings, our father was raping her. I knew something felt wrong; I just didn't know she was hurting. Rigel, they're hurting her!" she cried out.

I looked at the nurse. "Karen, can you give us some privacy? I got this."

The nurse hesitated before leaving the room and closing the door behind her.

I set my hygiene bag on the sink and dug inside it for soap.

"Can-can you call Jaliyah and ask her if my sister is okay? She feels anxious. Not scared, but angry. Please. Call her." Londyn looked up at me, watching me unbutton my shirt. She closed her eyes tightly, rocking back and forth under the shower water. "I think these niggas trying to set me up. Maybe I'm just paranoid," she sang to herself.

I undressed and got into the shower with her. I wasn't trying to make a move on shawty; I was trying to help her. Whatever she was experiencing, I just wanted her to know she wasn't alone. I grabbed her hands, lifting her from the floor. Her eyes were still closed tightly as if she didn't want to see me naked. I reached for the washcloth that was folded inside the indentation in the shower, and I placed my bar of Dove white in the washcloth. I looked Londyn in the face as I rubbed the Dove vigorously to create a lather under the shower water.

"Real ass bitch give a fuck 'bout a nigga. If she did, then she wouldn't be going city after city," Londyn sang.

I chuckled a little. Brielle played the fuck out of that *Slime and B* album that Chris Brown and Young Thug did together. She had that "City Girl" song on repeat some nights while she attempted to cook a nigga dinner. The only thing she knew how to cook was chicken alfredo and tacos. It wasn't like I wanted to have Moms over so much, but shit, after working sixteen hours some nights at the firm, I needed something besides chicken alfredo and fuckin' tacos. I knew how to cook, but I'd never cooked for Brielle. She didn't know I could even cook. She didn't ask me shit about myself for the most part. We looked good together. I was good for business.

"I knew when I started seeing Brielle that she had twin sisters," I told Londyn as I set the soap on the indentation in the tile. "I knew you were one of the twins," I admitted.

Londyn looked into my face as I placed the washcloth on her neck and applied a little pressure before I started washing her smooth skin.

"I saw you at a campaign event in Maryland when you were about seventeen. We lived in Maryland for a few years; that's how I ended up meeting you in the sixth grade. Anyway, my stepfather used to drag me to the campaign rallies with him. It was his way of networking with the rich politicians, looking for new clients for the family firm. I saw you with Kennedy Dupont. You looked uncomfortable as hell," I reminded her.

Londyn just looked at me, sighing as I washed her neck and shoulders firmly. She just listened as I told her how I found her.

"I attempted to make my way over to you, but you ended up getting lost in the crowd. When I got back home, I had one of Pop's investigators look you up. Found out you were adopted at two by the Cameron family. That you had an older sister and a twin and that you were engaged to Kennedy. You killed the nigga's mama at eighteen and was committed to that mental institution. I was trying to figure out my way to get back to you for years. Two years ago, I ended up looking for a private office outside of my stepfather's firm, and I looked up real estate agents. That's when I found your sister. I was with her for two years, and she'd never mentioned having a sister, let alone twin sisters."

"You're a fuckin' stalker." Londyn grinned a little, still looking me in the face. She hadn't even looked at my dick, and I didn't look her body over, either. I wasn't quite sure what that meant. I just knew I was happy I'd found her again after so long.

"A little." I grinned back.

"A *lot,* nigga. You dated my sister to get to me. You're sick." She was still smiling a little.

"You like sick, apparently," I reminded her.

"A little." She laughed.

"A *lot*." I looked her face over.

"Can you please call Jaliyah?" she asked again.

I nodded, handing her the washrag before grabbing one of my own. That was when we finally got a good look at each other's bodies. We didn't say anything; we just washed up and got out of the shower when we were finished. I had two outfits in my bag. Joggers, t-shirts, and slides for us both. I stuffed our clothes from the party back into my gym bag, and we waited for her to be discharged.

I had to make a quick stop on the way home. We left the hospital around 12:15 that afternoon. I bought Londyn some snacks for the two hour and fifteen-minute ride back to my place in Concord, a few minutes outside of Charlotte. As soon as the time on the dashboard of my E-Class hit 2:30, my phone rang. I laughed out loud, already knowing it was Knight calling to make sure I wasn't around shawty.

"You not gonna answer your phone?" Londyn snapped. I could feel her glare. "Must be one of your bitches."

"Nah," I assured her. "It's one of yours."

"Excuse me?" She sat up in the passenger seat, eying the number cascading across the screen on my console.

"Uncle Knight is trying to figure out why you're late for the 2:30 dick appointment. Guess he figured I was gonna run scared. He really thought I was gonna let you slide off with him and suck the nigga up or something." I frowned over at Londyn giggling to herself. "The nigga has a whole fuckin' wife."

"Yeah, the wife that *you're* fuckin'. Niggas cheat. That's what they do." Londyn rolled her eyes, shaking her head at me as I looked back out at the road. "I learned a long time ago that men separate their hearts and minds from their bodies. Love and sex don't go together for most men. They're territorial of their partner, though, for whatever fuckin' reason. You might think a nigga is yours, but the 'y' is definitely silent. They can cheat but let you get a number or smile too hard at a text that isn't from him. He be ready to stop the world from spinning and let everyone the fuck off. I learned the hard way when I got tired of white meat and wanted to try dark meat. Kennedy caught me fuckin' his driver. Swear that muthafucka slapped me so hard that my head turned in a full circle like that bitch on *The Exorcist*."

I drove through the gated community where I lived. While dating Brielle, I spent most of my time at her place. Until I stepped out on Brielle with Marley, I hadn't slept in my own bed in over a year. I'd go home from time to time to do some paperwork, but I didn't really like sleeping alone. I hated those long business trips I'd have to go on. I'd stay up days on end just so I could avoid sleeping alone. Every time I slept alone, I saw Shadow killing that man in front of my mom. I tried my best not to be anything like Shadow, but like him, I was silent and lethal when I was quiet. If I ever get quiet, I'm plotting my next move on a muthafucka, a move they'd never see coming.

"This you?" Londyn sat up straight as she eyed my four-bedroom, red river brick house.

She stared out the window in awe as I circled the driveway and stopped a few feet from the stairs that led to the front porch. I barely stopped the car before she opened the door to step out.

I didn't know why I felt so good around her. I'd only met the girl once in my life. Trap called me up that day she showed up at his hotel. He told me Gia wasn't acting like herself. Said he hadn't seen her in a year, but there was something different about her. He mentioned the fact that she kept calling him by his government name, something she'd never done. She had no remorse for fuckin' around with Knight, and she seemed excited by the fact that he probably looked like he wanted to snap her neck. I was leaving a client in Raleigh when he told me that his bodyguard's sister, Carmen, was taking her to the mall. I spotted them at the jewelry store. I could see that scar on Londyn's arm before I even approached her. Took everything in me not to grab that girl and kiss her.

"Nigga, you have a private pond?" Londyn exclaimed, walking through the grass toward my backyard.

I turned off the ignition and got out of the car, closing the door behind me. I watched her place her hand over her eyes like a visor to block the sun as she looked out over the pond.

She pointed to the lot of land to the left of my house. "You own this lot?"

I nodded, walking toward her. "Yeah."

"I want to buy it from you," she responded.

"You wanna... you wanna live next door to a nigga?" That caught me by surprise.

"I mean, Gia is going to need a place, and this place is beautiful. She doesn't need to go back to Trap. He didn't even know I wasn't her. Knight needs to stick with the wife he married. Gia doesn't need to pick up his pieces. She needs a fresh start right here on this land. I want to buy it for her, ya know, with my murder money. I added her name to my account so she has access when she gets out. It's money for her to spend while waiting for alimony from that rapper." She looked out at the empty lot as if she were mapping out its design in her head. "Four bedrooms. Her babies need separate bedrooms, and she can use the fourth bedroom for an art studio."

"She paints?" I asked.

Londyn thought for a moment. "I don't know. *I* do. I was hoping she did, too. We spent most of our time talking about what she wanted me to fix here in Charlotte. She wants me to leave her there, but I can't."

"I told you that I was going to make sure you're *both* free," I tried to tell her, but she wasn't trying to hear me.

"Nigga, the only thing I need you to sell me is this lot." She huffed. "I don't need you selling me a fuckin' dream."

"It's not for sale. My mother's family owns this land.

Mama's house is over there across the pond. The rest of the houses out here are my Nigerian relatives. I can't sell you the land, but I can build you a house next to mine. I wouldn't mind you as a neighbor." I watched her continue to roll her eyes.

"I don't need a handout, stalker. You know who the fuck my family is. I'm sitting on money that I'll never be able to spend in this lifetime, literally. They locked me away and threw away the key but couldn't touch my money. When I die, the shit will just be sitting there. I never had any kids; guess I'll leave it to Gia and her kids." Londyn sighed. She turned around and walked toward my house.

Just as I turned around to follow her, a Cadillac Escalade crept up my driveway. I grabbed Londyn's wrist and pulled her back so I could step in front of her as I pulled my gun from my waist. My eyebrows furrowed as I stared at the car as it pulled up behind mine.

"Who's that?" Londyn asked from behind me as I watched Marley step out of the car and close the driver's door.

I exhaled deeply, tucking my gun back in my pants. I didn't know how the fuck she found out where I stayed, but I was sure it was because my mother probably invited the girl over for dinner or some shit. Mama was always up to some shit. She wanted me with someone who resembled me. Didn't matter if I loved the girl or not. Didn't matter if the girl was married or not. A married woman was better than a light-skinned woman in Mama's eyes.

Marley walked toward us, and we met on my driveway, standing face to face. She looked at me long and hard before she looked at who she thought was Gia. "Gia..." She cleared her throat.

I wasn't sure if Londyn recognized whatever description Gia gave to her for how Marley looked. But from the guilt-stricken look on Marley's face, it didn't take Londyn five seconds to recognize the woman who told me Gia's exact whereabouts out of resentment. As soon as I heard Londyn cracking her knuckles, I stood in her way.

"Rigel, what is she doing here?" Marley asked. "She belongs in a mental institution!"

"Nah, bitch, *you* belong in a fuckin' mental institution!" Londyn tried to circle around me to grab a hold of Marley. "I bet you never expected to see me again, huh? You thought you got rid of me, huh? Getting rid of me *still* ain't gonna make that man love you, bitch! Fuckin' pick-me bitch! This bitch wanna be Gia so bad!"

"See," Marley shook her head. "She's delusional. Talking about herself in the third person again. Which crazy bitch are you today? Gabby or Megan?"

"I'm all three of us today, hoe, and all three of us are about to whup your fuckin' ass!" Londyn tried to push me out of the way.

I had to pick that girl up and throw her over my shoulder to get her away from Marley. As crazy as she was, she would probably choke Marley with her own dreadlocks. I carried her onto the porch, and she kicked and screamed the entire way.

I barely let her feet down to the pavement when she shoved me as hard as she could in my chest.

"Nigga, that bitch told you exactly where to find my sister! She sent my sister right back to the place where our own father was fuckin' her! Gia told her in therapy what was happening in that place! And she sent her back there!" Londyn shoved me again. "Get rid of this bitch, or I will."

I looked her in the face as I pressed the remote button on my keychain to deactivate my house alarm. I pressed the code on my front door, and the front door clicked open.

Londyn rolled her eyes at me before stepping inside. "Get Big Foot out of here. You better turn the page on this part of your life before I burn the entire book." She walked into my house, slamming the fuck out of the door like it was her fuckin' house.

I scratched my head, listening to my front door click. "You *do* know that this is *my* shit, right?" I scoffed before turning to walk off my porch toward Marley, who was standing beside her car.

"What is she doing here, Rigel?" Marley asked me as I walked up to her.

"Trap asked me to look after her while he is on tour. He wants to make sure she stays away from your husband, and your husband and his brother told me to stay the fuck away from her." I smirked a little as Marley folded her arms.

"You think this is funny? Brielle called me from the hospital after finding out her baby had been dead for days before she miscarried. She says that *I* knew and was keeping it from her! Frankie called me and said her mother gave some tea to *your* mother to give to her the night before she miscarried. You wanted this fight!" Marley watched the nonchalant look on my face. "Why would you want Shadow and Knight to come for you?"

"You have no idea what the fuck I've been through with my stepfather's family. They left a nigga to go through all types of pain that fuckin' money can't fix!" I let her know.

"Who is they?" Marley was confused.

"Your husband is my fuckin' uncle," I snarled. "And Shadow is my father."

Marley would have fallen if her car wasn't right behind her. She backed into her car, falling against it in shock. "Wh-what? How long have you known this?"

I just looked at her, waiting for her to figure out the answer to her own fuckin' question.

She laughed, still in shock. "You *always* knew. When you

met me that day at that party, you already knew who I was. You used me, Rigel? Is that what this was? I was all part of some plan to get back at the Shades for whatever you feel like they did to you? Or were you using me to find exactly where Gia was? Why me, huh?" She stood up from the car, staring me in the face, probably hoping to get some sort of response. "I cheated on my husband with you!"

"And your husband cheated on you with *her*," I reminded her and pointed toward my house. "We had fun. That was it."

Marley laughed out loud. "Fun, Rigel? *Fun?*"

"Why did you call me that night to tell me where Gia was? You caught her riding Unc's face, right? The nigga whose children you raise, whose house you clean, whose food you cook, whose dick you suck, married you but is fuckin' her. He's in love with *her*. And guess what, after knowing he's still in love with her, you're still in love with him, right?" I asked, watching her look the other way, ashamed that I was telling the truth. "Right?" I grabbed her chin, turning her face back toward mine to maintain eye contact.

She pushed my hand from her face. "He is my fuckin' husband!"

"Then go the fuck back to him and get the fuck off my property." I scoffed. "I didn't have to use you for information, by the way. You know that shelter over on Statesville Avenue? I run that shit. Y'all homegirl, Ginger, who helps with the SAFE program, is one of my volunteer nurses. She takes women from my shelter and moves them through that program. I've known about it since I started dating Brielle. What I didn't know until you told me the other night is that Shadow funds the program. And you only told me that information to get back at the people you feel hurt you. Go home."

"Gia is not well." Marley shook her head. "She's trouble.

Despite the fact that it wasn't her who killed those people, she needs help before she completely snaps."

"Well, maybe you better leave before she does." I frowned.

"Your mother invited me to dinner. I hired her on as a midwife. I had no idea of the dysfunctionality going on in this family. So, Shadow is your father? Your mother never mentioned—"

"He killed the man she loved right in front of her face after he fucked her in front of not just him but me. I was six years old watching that nigga fuck my mama before killing her new nigga. I went from seeing that shit to watching my stepfather pimp his own wife out to his friends to bring in clients. And she stayed for the fuckin' money. And you're staying with your nigga for a love that doesn't even exist." I tried to remain calm, but the more I thought about the fucked-up situation, the angrier I became.

"Are you coming to dinner?" Marley had the nerve to ask. She actually looked a little excited that she was getting under my skin. "Hey, I called your office looking for you, and your mama answered. She asked if I was hiring. Your family is rich, so it's definitely not about the fuckin' money. It's about the freedom."

"It's about pissing off Shadow," I corrected her.

"Same thing to a woman scorned." Marley looked me over before walking around to the driver's side. "Mama lives on the other side of the pond, right? It's beautiful out here."

I watched her get in the car and drive out of my driveway. I knew as soon as she saw Londyn at my place, she was going to let Knight know where she was. Marley was very easy to read. She was upset with her husband for lack of impulse control, but she was angrier at me for making her step out of her comfort zone.

I walked into my house, eyeing Londyn standing at the

sliding glass door in my dining room. She was looking out at the pond. I eyed my 60-inch television hanging on the wall over the fireplace. The television was turned to the news. The whole world knew Matthew Tiller and two of his bodyguards were both killed after a famous lawyer defended a rapper's wife from being sexually assaulted. I knew it would make it to CNN eventually. I had barely stepped into the house when my phone started vibrating in my pocket.

"I used your house phone to call Jaliyah's office. I didn't know niggas still used housephones," she said, still gazing out at the pond. "Gia got into a fight with the cafeteria lady over a brownie. Said her brownie wasn't big enough. That Gabby and Megan wanted their own brownie." She laughed to herself. "I knew then that Jaliyah knew Gia wasn't me. She said she was violating her patient's privacy by telling me, but she wrote in 'Londyn's' file that I was exhibiting signs of split personality disorder and schizophrenia. She asked me where I was and how I was doing. I told her I was in Charlotte, staying with a friend. I'm sure as soon as she gets a day off, she'll be up here. She knows better than to say anything over the phone. She's been my ride-or-die for the past nine years that I was in that place. She's been my dawg since we were kids. Speaking of kids, Trap's mama is going to fight for Gia's kids. I need you to help get her custody of her babies."

"You plan to leave the nigga who hired me to look after you?" I asked as I approached her side.

"Well, you *are* a lawyer, aren't you? So, start lawyering, nigga," Londyn said with all seriousness. "And I'm not Gia; *she's* who he hired you to look after. Gia wants a divorce, and she wants her kids back."

"First things first. Mama invited Marley to dinner." I looked her over from head to toe. Though she was in my gym clothes, her shape was still noticeable. Damn, she was fine. "I still have some of your sister's bullshit in the closet if you want to change. Y'all are about the same size, minus a few inches in your hips and thighs. You're thicker in that area than your sister."

Londyn rolled her eyes from the pond to me. "Nigga, don't fuckin' flirt with me. My sister is stuck in that nut house, and my best friend just realized we switched places. I'm hurting right now. The last thing I need is you being nice to me."

I laughed a little. "It's exactly what you need."

The tightness in her face loosened as she looked up at me. "You had me asshole-naked in the shower, and you didn't try to fuck me."

"There's more than one way to fuck someone, baby girl," I let her know.

There she was, rolling her eyes again and pushing me out of the way. "Nigga, let's go eat.

CHAPTER FIVE
MARLEY

"I'm honored to be a midwife for Shady Medical." Agnes smiled at me as I watched her set her dining room table for dinner.

"Yeah, until I work things out with the family, you'll be working with the women who are having home deliveries." I set a bowl of salad on the table. "You never mentioned to me that my brother-in-law is your son's father. That's something that, ummm, you should've brought up."

"Why?" Agnes scoffed. "Because you're screwing his son?"

I cleared my throat, watching her giggling to herself. "I'm not sleeping with your son. I am married to his uncle unknowingly. I don't see anything funny about this!"

Agnes disagreed as she walked over to a beautifully designed wine cabinet in the far corner of the dining room. "Actually, you should be laughing right now. Your husband just found out that the man you've been screwing is his nephew. He treated you like a game. Now you can show him how that game is played."

I watched her pull two bottles of champagne from the

refrigerated section of the cabinet. "I told your son where to find Gia so he could send her back to the psychiatric facility where she belongs. Turns out, another patient is the one who committed the murders. There are rumors on social media that she has a twin who killed those people. Regardless, they let her go, and she's back. Not back with my husband, but she's across the pond at your son's house! The same son who showed me affection that my husband has never shown me. And it hurts."

"Well," Agnes exhaled deeply, carrying the bottle over and setting it in a bucket of ice in the center of the dining room table, "at least now you and your husband will have a common enemy. A common enemy often mends broken relationships."

I shook my head, looking at all the food spread out over the table. A mix of soul food and Nigerian dishes. "I don't want to play this game," I told her.

"Too late to forfeit." Agnes laughed a little. "Shadow started this game when he shot the one man who actually heard me when I was silent. Shadow was too busy trying to learn the family medical business from my father. He wanted a different way of life than the drug game that his family had him living. It was his mother's death that opened the way for his family to start the multi-billion-dollar company he runs today. He should be thanking me."

My heart paused for a few seconds as I watched her pour herself some wine. "Thanking you? You played a part in having Knight's mother killed? I can't even make the man pancakes because of what happened to his mother! He was just six years old when he watched his father kill his mother!"

"And Rigel was only six years old when he watched his father rape me in front of the man who was supposed to be my husband! He killed him right in front of me and Rigel, and then he put his clothes back on and walked out the door like nothing ever happened. It was twenty-one years ago. It's time to heal and move the *fuck* on." Agnes smoothed down the edges of her expensive Brazilian lace front.

The doorbell chimed before I could even get the chance to ask her more questions about the horrible murders that both Knight and Rigel were forced to witness. I didn't know anything about Rigel's family. We didn't actually talk much about our personal lives other than the fact that my husband was fuckin' a mental patient and that his girlfriend left him the night of his anniversary because he'd accidentally fallen asleep. We confided in one another on Valentine's Day, and he was walking into that house with the same mental patient my husband was fuckin'. And why, I had no fuckin' idea.

"Another bitch with a pigment problem," Agnes muttered between her teeth before faking a smile as Rigel walked into the kitchen with Gia.

Rigel looked so good in his semi-casual polo shirt and plaid pants. Gia strolled alongside him in a copper satin maxi shirt dress. A brown belt snatched her waist, really accentuating the fact that this girl had the perfect fuckin' figure. The satin heels she wore made her legs look like they never ended. Her long, dark hair was draped over one shoulder. She looked so beautiful that I almost didn't notice her arm was bandaged.

"Mama, it smells good in here." Rigel went around the table to hug his mother.

"I thought you'd like something to eat. You know the women you attract don't know how to cook." Agnes glared at Gia over his shoulder before letting go of her son and smiling in his face. "Why is Gail here?"

Gia laughed out loud as Rigel went over and pulled out a chair for her. She grinned at him before smoothing out her dress as she sat down, and he pushed her chair in. "It's Gia. I know you must be hard of hearing at your old age."

"You better pray you look good at forty-two, Greta." Agnes scoffed.

I cleared my throat, walking around the table to sit opposite Rigel. I watched him slide into his seat next to Gia. The two assholes giggled, whispering to each other like they shared an inside joke or some shit.

"You know, I love that dress, Gia," I butted into their private conversation. "It kind of matches the chocolate diamond engagement ring that Rigel bought for your sister, Brielle."

Gia's light eyes brightened a little, something I'd never seen them do. She laughed a little, picking up her fork and examining it. "I'm no doctor or anything, but if I stab you in your external jugular vein with this polished fork, you'll bleed to death, right?"

"See. Belongs in the psych ward," I muttered to myself as I watched Rigel start to fix the girl's plate with the dishes that were closest to their side of the table.

"No, being psychotic is marrying a man who you know loves another woman. What the fuck did you think he was going to do to me when he finally got his hands on me? Don't be mad that your nigga is *our* nigga." Gia snickered.

Rigel nudged her. "Chill out." He frowned.

Gia rolled her eyes at him. "Nah, fuck her. Don't nobody want that nigga but her. I was just pissed off at Trap for putting me in that place. Knight doesn't know what he wants. One minute, he's talking about killing anyone who stands between him and his wife, and the next minute, he's knocking at my door, trying to make up for lost time. On Valentine's Day, he only fucked me because he saw you dancing at the skating rink with my sister's boyfriend." She shot Rigel a glare before glaring at me. "He only wants what he can't have. He doesn't like rejection. You'd know that if you knew your husband."

"Are we going to eat, or are we having Divorce Court?" Agnes snapped. "I invited Mrs. Shade over for dinner because she's hired me as a midwife for the Women's Clinic."

Gia's eyes quickly dilated as she gripped her utensils. "You made my sister that tea to expel the baby."

"The baby was already dead." Agnes rolled her eyes. "I was trying to help expel the damn demon. I was doing her a favor. She didn't need Shadow's evil spawn growing inside her."

Rigel looked at his mother as if he didn't like her choice of words. "Is that what you think of me when you look at *me*?"

Agnes' facial expression showed that she knew she'd fucked up when she insulted the DNA he also shared. "Brielle was supposed to be your fiancée, and she was pregnant by another man. Your father at that. I told you when you got involved with that white woman two years ago that she was trouble."

"White woman?" Gia asked.

"Yes, Michael Jackson, *white* woman." Agnes was not going to fix what she'd called Brielle.

"Oh, I get it." Gia giggled a little. "Rigel's father must've cheated on you with a light-skinned woman. Is that what happened? Matter of fact, that woman must've been your best friend, or else it wouldn't fuck with you this badly. If I didn't know any better, the nigga you were sneaking around with was probably that bitch's nigga. You seem like the type to play those types of twisted games".

Rigel and I both looked over at his mother. She looked upset by the words coming out of Gia's mouth, not because they were wrong, but because the guilty expression on her face let us all know that Gia was right.

"You don't want to fuck with me, Mrs. Gia Starr," Agnes warned her. "Your husband will end up canceling his tour to come rap at your funeral. Where are your children? I heard you have two babies. One baby who you tried to kill. And the other baby whom you shared a father with. According to your hospital records, one of your personalities actually liked fucking your father. I hope your mother-in-law never lets you see those kids again, you sick bitch."

Agnes barely got the last sentence out before Gia got up from the table and grabbed one of the steak knives. Rigel jumped up to grab her before she could go for his mother's throat.

"You evil ass bitch!" Gia screamed as Rigel tried to pry the knife from her hands.

"So, I've heard." Agnes snickered, fixing her plate like Gia wasn't about to slash her fuckin' vocal cords.

"Lonely, bitter bitches." Gia pushed Rigel off her and made her way out of the dining room. "Marley, tell ya nigga I'm running late for our appointment, but I'll be there in about an hour."

My nostrils flared watching that bitch leave the dining room.

Rigel sat back in his chair, frowning at the sound of the front door slamming as she left. "She has my key fob. I'm sure she's gonna find ya nigga wherever he is. Mama, you didn't have to aim that fuckin' low."

Agnes paused from eating her food to glare at her son like he'd lost his mind. "She went low, so I went lower. I can't help that your bitches are always sensitive. Must be the lack of melanin. She needs to worry about her sister in that hospital instead of worrying about my fuckin' business. Why is she here? You just broke up with her sister, you just fucked on your uncle's wife, and now you're trying to get *another* woman into your bed?"

"It's not like that with her." Rigel's jaws twitched. "I'm doing what I was paid to do. That's it."

"No, you're trying to piss off the Shades. Knight will be too busy worried about what Gia's doing with you to worry about mending his marriage with Marley, and Brielle will be too occupied with your involvement with Gia to concentrate on whatever she thinks she has with Shadow. You're stirring up more trouble!" Agnes tried telling her son, but for whatever reason, he wasn't trying to hear her.

Rigel grabbed a few items from the table and put them on the plate that was supposed to be Gia's. "Mama, I have bigger problems than other folks' marriage/relationship problems. I shot and killed a politician. They will fully investigate my involvement. Not to mention, they'll probably dig into your husband's company records just to fish for dirt on our family. And while the Tillers dig for dirt on us, I gotta dig for dirt on them. They play dirty, and I'm about to get muddy. So, while you're over here worried about who's fuckin' who, I'm worried about saving an innocent person's life."

I frowned, wondering what the fuck he meant by that.

His phone rang in his pocket. Frustrated, he dug into his pocket with his free hand. He frowned at the display on his phone before answering. "Yo? Nah, Trap, everything is cool. She's fine. You ain't gotta send Carmen back down here to watch over her. I got this. He's over and done, which is exactly what needed to happen." He looked at me and winked before walking out of the dining room with his new project's to-go plate.

"Did that nigga just take my good china to that white girl?" Agnes asked, reaching over the table to grab the bottle of champagne. She peeped the stunned look on my face as I sank back into my seat. "You need to figure out what brought on this sudden interest in that girl."

"It really doesn't feel sudden at all." I exhaled sharply,

picking up the champagne glass and holding it in the air so Agnes could pour me a glass.

"Here's to Knowles Realty. Congrats, Frankie, you did it, girl!" Grammy held up her wine glass at the official grand opening of Frankie's realty company. The company that was directly across the street from Brielle's company which still had the logo, 'Timing and Knowles Realty' on the front door.

None of the gang—Ginger, Spirit, Shiyah, and Jasmine—showed up to the grand opening that Saturday night. They were trying to stay loyal to Brielle. They knew she was sleeping with Shadow, but none of them knew the baby she was carrying was Shadow's. I only knew for sure that the baby was his because I saw Shadow asking the lab to run the DNA on the baby after Brielle had an amniocentesis done a few weeks ago. I was friends with everyone at the lab, not to mention I had access to thousands of client records. I knew before Brielle lost the baby whose baby it wasn't. Rigel knew himself that the baby wasn't his. He purposely got in the middle of Brielle and Frankie's friendship by becoming Shadow's lawyer. He won the case to piss off Frankie, not to help Shadow, his own father.

I actually thought things were going somewhere between Rigel and me. Yes, I wanted to mend my relationship with my husband, but if that failed, I thought I at least had Rigel to fall back on. I thought we were trauma bonding, but seeing him with Gia didn't seem like he was hurting from losing Brielle one bit. Or maybe he was just using Gia to make Brielle jealous. Who knew?

"You came!" Frankie's dark eyes lit up as I approached her with a bouquet of roses and a congratulations card that had a

$500 gift card to Coach enclosed. "Aww, for me? You shouldn't have!"

"It's a five hundred dollar gift card." I rolled my eyes as she snatched the card and then the roses.

"Well, in that case." Frankie smiled, smelling her roses. "You enjoying the party?" She looked around at the crowded office of people she barely knew. The only people in the room she knew were me and Grammy. The rest were probably clients and muthafuckas she'd handed out cards to while she was out club hopping.

"I don't know anyone here except for you and Grammy over there." I eyed Grammy over by the table of finger foods that I'd spent the previous night preparing for the event.

"Well, I invited the Hospital Hoes, but they all claimed y'all had some hospital convention tonight." Frankie thought for a second before looking at me. "If there was a hospital convention tonight, why are you here? You're here because there *is* no hospital convention. Wow. Brielle fucks my nigga and loses his baby, and *I'm* the bad guy because she lost an organ."

"They found a tumor, Frankie. She starts chemo once she's released on Monday." I watched the unbothered look on Frankie's face. "Her sister was just released from the psychiatric hospital, and she's staying with Rigel."

That Frankie responded to by frowning in confusion. "Why?"

I shrugged. "No idea."

"Does Brielle know?" Frankie watched me shake her head before she grinned devilishly. "Good. Why hasn't Gia gone to see her?"

"She's resting. She was attacked by her father earlier this week. The fact that she's been home for at least three days and hasn't seen her sister tells me she feels guilty about something. Maybe it's the fact that she left her sister in a mental institution." I started talking to myself as Frankie waved at a few people who were taking a plate to go.

Frankie faked a smile and slight wave before looking back at me. "Sister? In a mental institution? Wait, what did I miss? They threw Brielle in the nut house?" She looked a little too excited to think her former friend was a lunatic.

I pursed my lips, shaking my head at her. "Girl. No. They apparently have another sister who's locked away in Maryland. I've been calling Rigel all weekend. Apparently, he went up there to get Gia, and while he was there, he ended up killing a politician to save that girl. Too coincidental for me. Do you know anything about Gia?"

Frankie shrugged. "Shit, I didn't even know there *was* a Gia. I mean, I knew about Trap's wife. I've seen her all over social media, but I didn't know that she was Brielle's sister. She looks different without all that makeup she wears for the camera, but I knew she looked familiar when she came out of Brielle's back door that day after Knight. Why the fuck are you worried about that bitch with Rigel? You should be glad she's not with Knight." She shook her head at me, her braces gleaming under the office lights.

I agreed that I should've been happy. "Yeah, I should be, but why aren't I?"

"You want my mama to make her some tea? We know the recipes to get rid of everything, including her." Frankie tempted me.

I hesitated. "Nah, nah, that tea your mama made for Brielle was quiet enough. If the baby wasn't already dead, we would've been in serious trouble. If I'm reported to the medical board for knowing her baby was dead and not telling her, I'll ruin the credibility of the entire hospital. I paid her doctor not to tell her."

"Well, you know the Shades don't play fair." Frankie sighed

heavily, reminding me. "Shadow doesn't know I was involved, does he?"

I shook my head. "No. All fingers point to Rigel right now, and he doesn't seem to care."

Frankie turned to me, squinting her eyes as if she were looking at my facial expressions to figure out whatever she had in mind to ask me. "Why are you so concerned about Rigel?" Her eyes brightened as if a light bulb flicked on. "So that dance on the skating rink floor really *was* more than a dance? Rigel Worth is your fuckin' sneaky link? He's a cold ass lawyer who gave my baby-daddy custody of my kids, but the fact that you're fuckin' Brielle's nigga just makes me feel so much better."

I disagreed. "For one, I'm not fuckin' him anymore. It was a one-time thing."

Frankie looked at me as if to say I needed to play with somebody else because she was far from dumb. "Bitch..."

"Okay, maybe more than once." I rolled my eyes, "It's over now. We slept together. We vented to one another, and that was it. Him and Brielle were keeping secrets from each other, and it bothered him. He was hiding the fact that he was a private investigator looking for her sister. And Brielle was hiding the fact that she was running a non-profit escape route for battered women, which our company helps fund."

Frankie just stared at me like I was speaking a foreign language. "Say what now? An escape route?" Frankie eyed her guests, drinking and having a good time, not paying us any mind. She looked back at me, her eyes full of hurt and disgust. "What fuckin' escape route? She's a real estate agent."

I hated to tell her, "She runs a program to help transport women to safety all over the country, not to mention some programs in other countries. The Shade family has been helping fund her company. We provide food, shelter, money, transportation, and new identities. Shadow has been giving donations to her company for years."

Frankie laughed out loud. "And let me guess, the Hospital Hoes all know about this program, huh? I'm the only one who doesn't know. And I've known this girl since we were fuckin' kids! I didn't know she had sisters, didn't know she was fuckin' my nigga, didn't know she was Harriett Tubman, just didn't know shit! And I don't wanna hear the fact that she didn't tell me because she thought I'd run my mouth about whatever bitches she was helping. It's about the fact that *my* nigga is funding her shit! She's the reason Rigel fucked me over in court. He was trying to fuck her over because he probably knew she was fuckin' the nigga he was representing!"

Everyone always called Frankie "Ghetto Barbie," but they definitely couldn't call the girl dumb. I watched her set the flowers in a vase on the desk we were standing in front of. She was hurt. Everyone knew how she felt about Shadow. Even *I* knew, and I was just really getting to know the girl. She grabbed her shot glass from the desk, which was filled to the brim with brown liquor, and tossed it back before slamming it back on the desk.

"You see these people here?" Frankie nodded toward the people who were partying, having a good time. "Most of these people are Brielle's clientele, and the others go to some of her favorite restaurants. Some of these muthafuckas make more in one week than most of us will see in a year. I just put in five bids today for million-dollar beachfront properties for five of these people. As a real estate broker, I control my commission rate to an extent. On a million-dollar property, I make, on average, 60,000, and I'm about to sell five properties, bitch! Not to mention I hired those two girls over there flirting with that old rich nigga who has a hotel chain in the Midwest. I am working on taking most of Brielle's clientele. Her business will crumble, and she won't have shit to fall back on, but whatever non-profit shit she runs. I helped her build her business, and I'll definitely help tear it down."

The evil look in her eyes almost scared me, shit. Her type of hate was what I needed if I was going to figure out why Rigel took an interest in Gia. I didn't buy the shit about watching her for Trap. I didn't even buy the shit about pissing either Brielle or myself off. The way he looked at her let me know it was deeper. Sure, he was sensual with me, but the way he looked at Gia let me know he would stop the world for her.

"I'm thinking of taking a day trip tomorrow. Maybe head to Maryland in the morning," I thought aloud.

"Why?" Frankie asked.

"Well, Gia *was* my patient. I want to get her records personally. She already signed release forms while she was in my care, authorizing me to get her records. Yeah, she was 'Nicky Donn' on my records, but I can prove that Gia was in my care by showing copies of my notes that match what she exhibited at that hospital." I watched Frankie shake her head.

"If the signature says 'Nicky Donn,' they're invalid. You're a doctor, so you know that. You'd have to bring a family member with you to prove she was your patient, as in the bitch who was protecting her who's in the hospital herself right now." Frankie smacked her full lips. "What exactly are you trying to prove?"

"I don't know," I admitted. "Something. I'll figure it out when I get there."

"Well, let me know how it goes, shawty." Frankie laughed a little. "I'm about to party with these muthafuckas and make some more money moves. You can obsess about those bitches on your own. I'm not taking a trip to that zoo with you. If you really think Brielle can handle that type of shit, you gone 'head. She could barely handle watching *Girl Interrupted*. But have at it." Frankie blew me a kiss before walking off to join her party, bragging to folks about the gift card I'd just given her.

She was right, though. The way Brielle freaked out when Gia was on that floor at her place let me know she couldn't handle her sister's mental issues. She did, however, need to know she had a twin sister at a mental institution.

I tapped at Brielle's hospital room door that night. It was well beyond visiting hours, but of course, the nursing staff let me in to see her. It was around 10:30 that night, and I hadn't seen Knight all day. The kids were at my sister-in-law Sable's house. I couldn't be in that brand-new mansion alone with my thoughts. Something wasn't sitting right with me about Gia. She was definitely not the same Gia I knew. Yeah, the witty remarks and quick comebacks were there, but her demeanor was different. The Gia that I'd been reunited with the past two months was insecure and scared. The Gia I saw that day at Rigel and his mother's place was confident and fearless. A person didn't change that drastically in just a few days.

I walked into Brielle's room and eyed her sitting in the recliner in the corner of the room. There were three trays of damn food left in the room for her. "This fuckin' food service staff. They know better than this." I walked into the room, letting the door close gently behind me.

Brielle glanced at me as I went over to gather her trays and stack them on the sink. "Leave them," she said. "I'll eat them later."

"Hell no, Brielle. The shit is cold, and they should've taken each tray as they brought in a new one," I told her.

"What the fuck do you care? You sent my fuckin' sister to the mental institution over a husband who cheats on you after all you do for him!" Brielle cried. "I saw on the news that she's out! She's free, and the minute she's free, she's attacked by her father! The same father who was raping her in that place for a whole fuckin' year! He found her because of you!"

I shook my head. "I think she might have been looking for him. That's the only way to explain Rigel being in the hotel room with her that day."

Brielle looked at me as I went over and sat on the sofa adjacent to the recliner she sat in. "The reporters say Rigel was at that hotel because of a campaign party. You know the Worths always host those events. He saved her."

"Her?" I laughed a little. "Her of all people? The entire reason Gia was arrested that day was that I told Rigel where to find her! The surgical staff told me that night that she was singing you to sleep before surgery, and I told him where to send the police! Trap hired Rigel as a private investigator. He'd been looking for your sister the entire time, to turn her in, not to fuckin' protect her! Do you even know how your sister's case was dismissed?"

Brielle's light eyes searched mine for answers. "How?"

"Someone else committed those murders. Haven't you been on social media? They're saying Gia has a twin sister in that place!" I exclaimed.

Brielle sank back in her recliner as if she was thinking. "I can remember all the way back to age two. The memories are blurry and scattered, but I can remember back that far. And I do remember it being three of us, but it's fuzzy. The last memory I had of there being two Gias was when I was about four. The memories after that only include Gia and me. I remember calling the other one Lu-Lu."

I looked at her as she thought aloud. "So, there *is* a twin!"

Brielle frowned, looking at me. "And?"

"Don't you want to see her?" I asked.

Brielle hesitated. "At the psychiatric facility? Gia's here somewhere with her arm cut the fuck open. Nurses say she's coming Monday to pick me up!"

"I can get you released tomorrow morning to take a trip to visit your sister. I mean, she hasn't seen you in twenty-five years. Gia has a lifetime with you. You don't even know your other sister's name. She's got life at that place. She's never getting out. Don't you think she'd like to see her big sister?" I questioned. "I'm going there to try to get Gia's records. She needs help regardless of if she was set free, and you know it. She's technically still under my care, regardless of whether she is still in your program or not."

"If there even *is* a program anymore." Brielle shook her head. "Ginger called a few minutes ago saying that Frankie posted on social media that I had some sort of secret women's rescue mission going on! I've been running this company for years undetected, and all of a sudden, she knows! Do you think Rigel told her? I mean, she's cool with his mother! He's probably the one who had her making that fuckin' tea for me! And you knew the baby was dead and didn't even tell me!"

I knew that would come up. I had to come up with something to tell the girl. "Your doctor approached me, telling me that there was no fetal movement and the heartbeat was faint. That doesn't always equal fetal death. As far as the tea is concerned, there was a mix-up with the batches that Frankie's mother, Uma, made. Her mother makes teas that help assist with unwanted pregnancies. What would I gain by helping you pass a dead baby?"

"You wanted me to blame Rigel." She sat up in the chair. "You wanted me to be angry at him so he could go back to you. How long were you fuckin' him?"

"Not as long as you were fuckin' Shadow," I let her know.

She laughed a little, grimacing in pain as she reached over

her chair to pull the lever to let the footrest on the recliner back down to the floor. "You fucked Rigel because my sister was fuckin' Knight."

"I didn't know he was your boyfriend until the new year," I tried telling her. "He'd mentioned he knew you were a real estate agent who ran the SAFE program. And that he knew you were running that program the entire time." I watched her nodding, probably thinking that it sure was him who told Frankie when I was the only person he'd mentioned it to. "That's how I put two and two together and came up with Brielle Timing. Until then, I had no idea he had a girlfriend. Gia is staying at his place."

Brielle looked at me, her nostrils flaring. "He's trying to turn my sister against me."

I hesitated. That wasn't what I expected to hear, especially since the Gia I knew loved Brielle. Frankie said she thought Gia was gonna jump on her when she came flying out of Brielle's back door that day. Gia was fearless when it came to protecting Brielle. The entire time the police were trying to drag Gia out of the hospital on the day Brielle had surgery, Gia was screaming that she couldn't leave Brielle.

And there Brielle was, quick to switch sides over a nigga.

"Yeah, I'll take that trip." Brielle nodded. "How soon can you have me checked out of here?"

I picked Brielle up the next afternoon at around 1:30 p.m. She was still very sore from the hysterectomy and really shouldn't have been taking a road trip, no matter how much I needed her to get those records for me on her sister. But when we got to Baltimore that night, the records department was already closed despite the fact that the woman on the phone said someone would be there until 9:00 to help me. We got to Baltimore around 7:30 that night, and there was no one at the records department. Not to mention, visiting hours were already over.

Brielle was too weak to be upset. She went over and sat in one of the chairs in the waiting area to catch her breath and take her meds to ease her pain. I stood at the empty receptionist's desk, frustrated as hell because I needed answers.

"Ummm, can I help you? Visiting hours are over."

I looked up to see a pretty brown-skinned girl approaching me. She looked like a cute school teacher with her glasses, messy bun, crisp white blouse, and high-waisted knee-length skirt. She pranced toward me in gray pumps, clipboard in her hands.

"Hi." I put on a smile as she stood before me. "I'm Dr. Marley Shade. I'm here—" I barely got the words out before she covered her mouth, trying to keep from screaming.

"*You're* a Shade?" she squealed, removing her hand from her mouth, her eyes big as coasters.

I shook my head before nodding, remembering that I *was* a Shade. "No, I mean yes. I'm married to Knight Shade. I help run the—"

She was pretty much grabbing me to hug me then like a fan. "Oh my goodness! I'm Dr. Jaliyah Marcus! I've read all of you and your husband's work! I've read all his case studies and have even put my patients on similar medications as his patients!" She was so excited to be in my presence. Her smile faded when she saw Brielle on the couch, hunched over in pain. "Who is that?" She looked back at me.

"Gia Starr's sister, Brielle Timing. She wants to meet her sister. She's never met Gia's twin. I thought I'd bring her here to meet her while I was getting Gia's records," I told her.

That light in Jaliyah's eyes dimmed as she looked my face over. "I saw Gia on the news. Her father attacked her. Is she okay? I guess she didn't want to ride with you two and come back to this place. I knew her twin was here, but the staff kept what was happening to her to themselves. I never knew she was being raped until her sister told me what was going on. The institution is being investigated as we speak, which is why we're short-staffed. I was staying over, helping out the nurses on duty." She walked past me and over to where Brielle was sitting.

Brielle's face was buried in her hands as she moaned in pain.

"Honey, are you okay?" Jaliyah rubbed Brielle's back.

"I had a hysterectomy," Brielle mumbled, groaning in pain, hands still covering her face.

Jaliyah gasped and looked over at me like I'd lost my medical fuckin' mind. "She should be on bed rest! Come on, honey. I can take you to get some ice packs. Are y'all coming from Charlotte? No way you drove this girl six hours like this!"

"I wanted to see my sister." Brielle removed her hands from her face, her eyes puffy and tired. "Please, take me to see her. I don't even know her name. I can't remember her name."

Jaliyah frowned a little as if she wasn't even sure she wanted to say Gia's twin's name in front of me. As if she didn't trust me to say the girl's name. She carefully helped Brielle up from the chair. "Come on, hun. I can get you back to see your sister. Visiting hours are over, but I'll make this exception for *family*." She shot me an angry glare before helping Brielle through the lobby. "Dr. Shade, wait here."

CHAPTER SIX
BRIELLE

I didn't believe for one second that the girl who came back to Charlotte was Gia. No way she'd be anywhere near Rigel after what his mama did to me unless she didn't know Rigel. I wasn't sure how the twins pulled it off, but I knew in my heart that whoever came back to Charlotte couldn't be the sister who sang me into a deep sleep before I went into surgery. Marley was the last person I trusted, but she had the authority to get me discharged from the hospital.

Shadow had been smothering me since I entered the hospital, and I was just glad to get some air from him. He'd been acting strangely ever since he left Raleigh after going with Knight to see my sister. Knight felt some type of way about Rigel being there with Gia, and from the looks of things, Marley did, too. She wasn't slick; I knew she had some sort of motive for taking me to see my long-lost twin sister.

"How's Gia?" Jaliyah rushed over behind the nurse's station to grab an ice pack and wheelchair for me to sit in.

I shrugged a little, arms wrapped around my stomach. "She

hasn't stopped by to see me at the hospital. She was injured and is supposed to be resting up herself."

"I'm just concerned about her mental state." Jaliyah helped me into the chair and placed the ice pack on my abdomen. "I was only Gia's psychologist for about a week before she escaped from the facility a few months ago, but I reviewed her file. She was put in The Bayou after trying to kill herself and harm her baby. She apparently suffered from postpartum psychosis, which was never treated. And since it was never treated, it caused her split personality disorder and schizophrenia to progress."

I eased down into the chair, and relief washed over me as she wheeled me down the hallway of the facility. I had an eerie feeling being in that place. If crazy had a smell, I'd say it was that place. It smelled like prunes, penicillin, bandages, and fruit snacks. As Jaliyah wheeled me down the hallway, patients stared at me through the glass in their doors. One of them even mouthed, "You better run," while I passed by.

"Dr. Marcus—"

"Call me Jaliyah." Jaliyah extended a welcoming voice.

"Jaliyah," I corrected myself. "Did you know my sister was being raped in this place?"

Jaliyah hesitated. "Everyone heard about it, but it *is* a mental institution, and Gia wasn't exactly the most reliable witness. Yet and still, it should've been investigated. Matthew Tiller has several family members working here, including the nurses who allowed him in after hours and the security guards who were killed. The twins' family members worked here, not to mention Londyn's foster family, the Camerons, own this facility. Her husband's family, the LePonts, donate millions to the facility, and so do the Tillers. Money trumps mental patients claiming rape allegations. It's wrong, but that's how it goes in a place like this."

"Londyn," I sighed at the sound of my sister's name. "My mama just gave away *one* of her twin babies?"

"From what I found out, she tried to give the family *both* babies, but they only wanted one." Jaliyah wheeled me onto an elevator at the end of the hallway. Once on the elevator, she pressed the basement button. "What are you doing here with Marley Shade?"

I sighed deeply. "At one point, I thought I could trust her. She's done a lot for an organization that I run. She genuinely cared about the women I tried to help until one of those women was Gia. The two have a history that I know nothing about to this day."

"Marley should've never been her doctor." Jaliyah huffed.

"I mean, I had no idea they even knew each other when Gia entered my program. I definitely had no idea she was fuckin' the woman's husband. Gia was fuckin' her nigga, and Marley was fuckin' mine. And I was fuckin' Frankie's whatever-he-was." I thought about all our karmas. Neither of us had any room to judge the next when we were all doing some fuck-shit.

"Well, Gia is on new medication and doing just fine," Jaliyah let me know as the elevator quickly moved down the shaft. "There's a reason why Marley brought you here. She wants to visit Gia's twin for some answers or maybe some suspicions. Make sure when you leave here, you take my number and let me know as soon as you get in touch with Gia."

The elevator stopped abruptly at the basement floor, and we got off. My heart was pumping at full speed as Jaliyah rolled me off the elevator. She wheeled me down a long hallway with rooms that had steel doors. The doors looked heavy like they were trying to keep monsters contained.

"How-how long has Londyn been here?" I gulped.

"Here in the facility? Since she was eighteen. Down here in The Dungeon? Since she started injuring patients and staff and sleeping with the staff for favors." Jaliyah laughed a little to herself. "You'd be surprised by the things she'd do or let the guards do to her for a pack of cigarettes or a blunt. Male *and* female guards, not to mention a few of the nurses and CNAs. For the past few days, though, Londyn hasn't said much of anything. She just sits and stares at the television or sits in front of the radio. I don't know when she last had some sleep. It's almost as if she's afraid to go to sleep. The amount of meds she's on should tranquilize her, but they're doing the exact opposite."

Jaliyah stopped in front of a room that had two guards standing outside it. She nodded at them both before one of them entered a code on a keypad. The lock released, and the door crept open. One of the guards held the door open so Jaliyah could wheel me in. Once inside, I choked back tears at the sight of my sister sitting on the bed, staring at a television that wasn't even on.

"Londyn?" I whispered yet spoke loudly enough for her to hear me. When she didn't budge, I called out, "Gia?"

Whoever she was, she looked at me and rolled her eyes a little before looking back at the blank television screen. "Gia's somewhere with your nigga," she snapped.

Definitely sounded like Gia, but I still wasn't exactly sure.

"Are Londyn and Gia identical?" I asked Jaliyah as she walked around the wheelchair over to a vanity mirror, which had all of my sister's hygiene products. Her room almost looked like a hotel suite instead of a room in a nut house.

"As identical as identical can be. There are very subtle differences. Have to really know them well to notice. How well do you know Gia?" Jaliyah scoffed as if she was actually calling me out.

"Not as well as I should, but that's not entirely my fault. I looked for Gia for years. Even reached out. I didn't know she was sick. I had no idea what she was going through, and she had no idea what I was going through after our mother was killed, either." I told whichever sister that was sitting on that bed. "Or what Londyn went through with her foster family."

My sister didn't look at me. She just watched Jaliyah go over to grab a detangling brush. Gia's thick, curly hair sat on top of her head like a nimbostratus cloud. She looked just like Gia, *too* much like Gia—like she *was* Gia. Jaliyah had been around the twins, and she acted as if it was Gia. She was their doctor. There's no way she'd let the twins switch places. Right?

"Why was Londyn sent here?" I asked Jaliyah, even though Londyn was supposedly sitting in my face.

"Well," Jaliyah grabbed some detangling spray before she walked back over to sit behind my sister on the bed. She started combing Gia's curls. "She killed her mother-in-law. Her foster family owns this facility. They paid for the best lawyers to have her committed. She's here for life. Entire life gone. No kids. No family. No freedom. She never got the chance to live, and she's gonna die in this place." Jaliyah's eyes watered as she brushed through my sister's hair. "It's not fair," she whispered. "She never got the chance to feel love or affection. I've always wanted that for her."

"How long have you been her psychiatrist?" I questioned.

She looked at me before looking back at my sister's hair. "I've been her psychologist for just a few years. She talks about her sisters almost every day. I was told not to tell her about Gia once she was committed. They didn't think it was a good idea to reunite the twins. The same day Londyn found out about Gia was the same day she found out their father was being let in to tranquilize and rape her. She said she had to put an end to Gia's pain. She said, 'Somebody has to put an end to this.' The staff made sure to not bring it up when I was around, so I had no idea what was going on. When Gia came to me and tried to tell me her father was raping her, I should've listened. I thought she was pregnant by one of the staff members. Had no idea that the baby was her father's. How *are* the children, by the way?"

My sister finally looked my way as if to ask the same question.

I hesitated. "I-I wouldn't know. With Trap's mother while he's on tour, I'm assuming."

"Some fuckin' big sister," my sister muttered, smacking her teeth before staring back at the TV.

"If I know Gia, she's got a plan to get her kids back. She wants a normal life. She's tired of being mentally locked in a prison. She's tired of pain. Whatever you do, keep her away from that woman in the lobby," Jaliyah warned me.

My sister frowned in confusion. "Woman in the lobby?" she hesitated to question.

"Marley Shade is out there." Jaliyah huffed.

My sister's eyes widened before she glared my way. "The same bitch who Gia says is the reason you were poisoned? You almost bled to death!"

I shook my head, holding the ice pack over my abdomen. "The baby was already dead. The tea only put me in the hospital to face the inevitable, that my baby was dead and that I couldn't have any more children. I start chemo soon because they found a tumor and removed my uterus. For whatever reason, Agnes wanted to cause a problem between her son and the Shades. She wanted my children's father to think her son killed my baby."

"You came to this place with one of the Shades." Jaliyah scoffed. "She didn't tell you what was going on between the families? She didn't tell you why a woman would want someone to come after her own son?"

"The only thing I know is my sister came back from

Raleigh with her arm cut open because her father tried to assault her, and Rigel killed him. He rescued my sister, and she's made a new friend. Rigel was just fuckin' Marley, and now he's Gia's hero." I rolled my eyes, sinking back into the wheelchair.

My sister grinned a little before looking back at the television like it was on. "Marley must *love* that." She laughed mischievously along with Jaliyah.

The fuck kind of psychiatrist is this? I thought. The two sat there giggling like best friends plotting on an enemy together. Like they didn't just hear me say that our own sister was somewhere with my ex-boyfriend. Marley had no room to be mad at Rigel for being around another woman. The only reason she'd even come back to the facility was to dig into Gia's records, but it backfired on her. Jaliyah pretended to be starstruck until she saw me in the lobby and realized Marley was trying to use me to get to her patient. By the looks of how she sat brushing my little sister's hair, the twins may have been more than just patients to her.

"How long did you say you've known Londyn again?" I switched the subject as their laughter subsided.

"Does that really matter?" Jaliyah looked at me like I had some nerve.

I nodded. "It kind of does. You'd know the difference between Gia and Londyn, which is why I'm asking. The Gia I know wouldn't go anywhere near my ex, regardless of him saving her life."

"The Gia you *know*?" Supposed-to-be-Londyn frowned. "How well did you really know Gia? She told me that you barely talked to her while she was in Charlotte. That you treated her like one of your clients instead of a sister. She only clung to Knight because she couldn't cling to you. She was barely holding on; she was drowning, and you just watched her sink. She didn't need a psychiatrist. She needed a fuckin' sister."

The words stung. She was definitely not wrong, whichever twin she was. I had no idea that Gia was suffering all those years. All I focused on was the fact that she never reached out. It wasn't until I saw her in a psychotic episode in the corner of my dining room that I realized she'd been through something traumatic. Everyone handles pain differently. I'd gotten help for my mental scars over the years. Her mental scars turned into something much more. I was sitting in that wheelchair, witnessing one of the twin's mental scars. I wasn't quite convinced that she was Londyn, and she was right—I didn't know enough about Gia to think the twin in my face was Gia, either. And looking at the connection she had with Jaliyah, I wasn't too convinced that muthafucka didn't know they switched places.

"Well, whichever twin she is, she needs to stay the fuck away from my ex," I told them both. "I didn't do right by Gia by making her feel unwelcome when she came to me for help. And I didn't do right by Londyn by not looking for her when I remember there being three of us when we were younger. I remember her. I used to call her Lu-Lu. I played with her. I laughed with her. I told everyone that Lu-Lu and Gi-Gi were *my* babies. And I just forgot about one of them when Mama started losing her mind. I remember there were three of us, then one day, there were just two. And Gia was so sad. She hasn't been the same since."

The twin sitting on the bed glanced at me. Her eyes glossed over before she quickly looked away. "When you see Gia," she choked back, "can you repeat everything that you just said? I know she needs to hear that, too. She thought you forgot about her. She thought *we* forgot about her. Tell her that you didn't forget her. Please."

I watched a tear fall from her eyes. As I started to respond to her wishes, the door to the room opened. One of the guards who was standing in front of the door stepped inside.

"Time's up," he growled, looking at Jaliyah and me. "The mental patient is on restriction, and Dr. Marcus, you know they send people here every hour to walk around the institution to make sure no one unauthorized is in the building. Get her out of here. And you should go home for the night."

Jaliyah patted my sister on the back before getting up from the bed. "I will be here first thing in the morning," she assured my sister.

I took one last look at the twin before Jaliyah came over to me, turning my chair around so we could walk out the door.

As we were leaving, my sister called out to me.

"Hug Gia for me, will you?" she whispered.

"So," Marley hesitated to ask once we were in the car early the next morning, headed back to Charlotte. "What did you think of the twin?"

I rolled my eyes from the road to her, then back to the road. We'd stayed at a hotel overnight, getting rest for the drive back home. I got a room as far away from hers as possible, on a completely different floor. I didn't want to be anywhere near her. If I was more mobile, shit, I would've taken the train back to Charlotte or even caught a damn hour and thirty-seven minute flight. We'd been driving a good five hours and a half hours when she finally decided to say anything to me besides whether or not I wanted something from the gas station.

As soon as we got in the car, I popped my meds and went the fuck to sleep. I was enjoying the sound of *not* hearing the bitch's voice when she decided to open her mouth. We only had about an hour left; she couldn't continue the silence until then? Damn.

"Which one?" I muttered.

"The one at the Bayou." Marley mocked my monotone. "Your long-lost sister. The one who's locked away while you and the other one are free."

"Have you *met* Gia?" I laughed out loud. "She's far from free. Her mind is very much caged."

I wasn't so sure the twin with Rigel was even Gia. I wouldn't know for sure until we were face to face, and even then, I might not even recognize her. I hadn't spent enough time with Gia to even know the difference. And for that, I was ashamed. Very ashamed. Regardless, I wasn't going to tell Marley that I had doubts. She was up to something. The bitch had set Gia up once before; I wasn't going to let her do it again.

"What's the twin's name?" Marley had the nerve to ask me.

"Her name is drive back to Charlotte." I rolled my eyes. "We went there to get whatever records you wanted for Gia, and that was an epic fail. They're finally investigating that place after an entire year of him raping my sister. It took his death for the police to actually look into that shit. I'm sure the Tillers are trying to find a way to say my sister seduced that soggy saltine cracker. There is no reason why you need my sister's name after you reported my fuckin' sister! You set her the fuck up! But she's free now, and with your nigga who's not your nigga." I smirked.

Marley gripped the wheel.

"Yeah, it doesn't take a rocket scientist to know you were fuckin' my man. Y'all were basically fuckin' on the skating floor at Roll Up!" I exclaimed. "Got some nerve turning my sister in when *both* you and Knight are cheating on each other! You wanna know why Rigel is with Gia? Ask the nigga because I'm sure gonna ask my sister. She's got a husband out on tour, who somehow got my number while I was in the hospital and has been blowing my shit up all week. She's probably got Knight wondering why she's with a nigga whose mama could've made me bleed to death. And she's got you wondering if she's who she says she is, which is why you took me with you to that institution, huh? You wanted me to see if I could tell the difference between the twins?"

Marley glanced at me before looking back at the road. She was trying to read me but couldn't. She knew I was a real estate broker. I was a salesman. I could convince an Eskimo to buy a house on the beach; I was so good at pitching. Marley couldn't tell if I knew the difference between the twins or not. All she knew was that regardless of who the twin with Rigel was, I didn't want her anywhere near him. Not after the pain he'd caused and after the pain he was definitely about to cause.

Just as Marley was about to turn the music up so we could end our conversation and drive the remaining hour to Charlotte, her phone rang. Shadow's name cascaded across the display on her console.

"*Fuck,*" I muttered.

Marley answered. "Yes, brother?" She rolled her big, pretty eyes.

"Why the fuck are you and Brielle in Lexington?" Shadow's voice resonated through her speakers.

I exhaled sharply, remembering that even though my phone was on Do Not Disturb, Shadow still had my damn location.

He didn't even let Marley explain. "She just had a fuckin' hysterectomy, and she starts fuckin' chemotherapy on Wednesday. You're a fuckin' doctor; you know she'll have a fuckin' setback if she doesn't follow the surgeon's orders. You're about ten minutes from my place on Nautical Winds Drive. Bring her to me fuckin' now."

You heard daddy. I smirked.

I shouldn't have been so happy that Shadow was upset. Because just like he went off on her, as soon as we pulled into his peaceful mansion overlooking High Rock Lake, he was waiting on his front porch, ready to go the fuck off like someone's daddy upset that his daughter came in past curfew.

Marley got out of the car as Shadow approached. "Shadow, wait. Let me explain. I—"

"How the fuck did the cops know where to get Gia?" Shadow questioned Marley.

Stunned that he'd asked her the question, she immediately went into defense mode. "As doctors, we are obligated to tell the authorities if one of our patients is a fuckin' murder suspect! The reputation of *your* family's hospital is at stake here!"

"Nah, you saw your husband fuckin' that patient, so you put her back in the same facility where her fuckin' father was raping her! That little baby she came here with is her father's. Did you know that? The shit is all over the fuckin' news! If you never sent the girl back there, her father would've never gotten the chance to attack her again and—"

Marley looked into his face as he stopped himself from talking. She looked back at me, sitting in the car listening to their conversation, waiting for Shadow to explain why he was so upset. She looked back at him.

"Oh, right, you're feeling some type of way about Rigel. It's okay. It's the Worth family who will be investigated. Why would you be worried about a Worth being investigated? What Rigel does doesn't fall back on you. I mean, it's not like you're his father." Marley laughed a little, watching Shadow's face ball into a frown. "Get the girl's bag out of my car and help get her inside. Clean up *your* messes, and don't worry about mine."

Shadow was dressed in a white t-shirt, his plaid lounge

pants, and his old man slippers. He only wore that outfit when he had his children with him. I knew those boys were driving him insane. Those two were the black *Children of the Corn*, I promise you. Shadow walked his grumpy ass over to my side and yanked the car door open.

I glanced at Marley as she slid into the driver's seat, shutting her door behind me. She rolled her eyes at me a little as Shadow reached for my overnight bag on the floor. He put the strap over his shoulder before reaching across me to unbuckle my seatbelt. Before I could even object to him helping me, his big, strong, sexy, muscular ass lifted me out of the seat. I wrapped my arms around his neck as he pulled me from the car.

Shadow frowned into my face as he backed into the passenger side door to close it.

He barely got the door closed before Marley's bitch ass was skirting out of the driveway and off his land. "You're supposed to be here with me today, yet you're with *that* bitch. I went to the hospital to check you out when they told me that Marley checked you out yesterday. You just had major surgery. What were you thinking?" He carried me toward his house, a house I'd never been to.

I looked into his face, taking in the crisp air around us. The cool air from the lake actually felt good. I'd just lost my fuckin' uterus and was already having fuckin' hot flashes. "I wanted to see my twin sister, who probably thinks I abandoned her, too."

"Gia was leaving the hospital when I was walking in." Shadow carried me up the stairs and into the house. He gently let me down to the floor and set my bag alongside the coat tree in the corridor.

I looked at him as he watched the way I held my stomach. I was in so much pain. "I need to—"

Shadow wrapped his arm around my waist and led me

toward the living room, where he sat me down on his comfy gray sofa. Just as he sat me down, both his sons came rushing by, laughing and giggling with a Bully puppy.

"We came out here for a little while to get away from everything. Things are hectic an hour away in Charlotte," Shadow told me what I already knew. "Frankie is blowing up my fuckin' phone, coming down to the clinic, telling my staff I gave her syphilis. She's all over social media talking about an 'underground DV shelter' and shit. Not to mention Gia's kicking it with my—"

I looked at Shadow, my heart having a feeling that something was off before I knew. "Gia's kicking it with your who?"

Shadow sat beside me on the couch. "I had no idea he was my son. I hadn't seen him since he was six years old."

"Who?" I didn't want to think he was talking about Rigel, but the hurt expression on his face let me know Rigel was exactly who he was talking about. "Rigel is your son?"

"I haven't seen him since he was six," he repeated. "Last time I saw that boy, I killed his mama's new nigga in front of him. Did something I shouldn't have to his mama in front of him, too. And to get me back, she told my crazy father where to find my mother. If I would've touched her, her father would've killed my whole fuckin' family. And there would've been a war between the Falls and the Shades. She changed his name, and I lost track of him. The last I'd seen the nigga, his name was Winter Shade."

I looked over at his kids playing with the dog, laughing hysterically at the dog who was nibbling at their feet. Those little boys were Rigel's half-siblings. No wonder Agnes took an interest in that girl. It wasn't because Frankie was Nigerian. It was because her children were her son's siblings. I looked back at Shadow, who sank into the back of his chair.

Rigel had a rough childhood being raised by the Worths. It

was pretty much an arranged marriage. His mother was considered worthless for having a baby and not being married. They paired her with a man whose wife died giving birth to her fourth child. Agnes raised his four children as her own, often neglecting Rigel. His stepfather made Agnes sleep with his father so he'd inherit the family business. His stepfather's brother sexually assaulted him when he was eight. He didn't want to tell his mother, so he told his grandfather. A few days later, the pervert was found dead behind a church. Rigel held onto Shadow's watch like it was worth his soul, saying it was all he had left of his father. He couldn't believe Shadow left him to fend for himself.

I wanted to be angry at Shadow, but it had been twenty-one years. He was young.

"It was a long time ago," was all I could think to say.

I didn't want to dive too deep right then and make the man feel worse than I was sure he already felt. I was cheating on my boyfriend with his father, and his father was fuckin' on his son's girl.

"I'm in love with my son's ex." Shadow laughed to himself. "And my son fucked his uncle's wife. Ain't this some bullshit?"

"A bullshit!" the two-year-old Stratus repeated after his father.

"What did I tell you about fuckin' cussin'?" Shadow huffed.

"You said… You said you'd beat my ass if I don't stop." Stratus giggled.

"Ass," one-year-old Cloudy repeated.

"Karma is a muthafucka." Shadow turned to me. "Rigel purposely sought out Gia's husband to find her. He knew Knight's connection with her. He's playing on her guilt. She feels responsible for what happened to you because she was fuckin' around with Knight. Get your sister away from that nigga as soon as possible. He'll do anything to hurt us, including hurting her to get to you."

I hesitated. I don't know why, but I didn't feel he wanted to hurt Gia. Shit, I didn't even know if the chick he had with him was even Gia. Shit, Knight would know if she was the woman he loved. I wasn't sure what depths Rigel would go to in order to keep Knight away from Gia, but Knight would definitely know whether she was the same woman.

"Was Gia with Rigel when she was leaving the hospital? I'm sure he took her there to pick me up," I questioned.

Shadow frowned a little. "He was waiting for her outside, alongside that clean sports car of his. He held the door open for her, and she hopped in."

"Did she look like she was in danger?" I had to ask.

"The fuck does that have to do with anything? He's with my brother's woman, Bri!" Shadow watched me shake my head.

"Knight's *woman*, who is his *wife*, just dropped me the fuck off at this beautiful house on the lake. Gia is not his woman because he's fuckin' married," I reminded him.

No, I wasn't excited about Rigel getting in my sister's head, but I needed him to occupy her time while I figured out whether she was Londyn or not. Because if she *was* Gia, Rigel was playing with fire. And if she was Londyn, she'd escaped a mental institution where she was committed for life. If Marley found out, neither of my sisters would ever get out of that place. I didn't know what I was more afraid of—Knight killing a nephew he barely even knew or Marley setting up my family again.

"The nigga took me on as his client to fuck up your friendship with Frankie." Shadow tried to place the blame on Rigel again.

"No, *I* fucked up my friendship with Frankie." I had to take accountability. "That girl is in love with you, and I've known that from day one. She may have just been sex to you, but you are the man to whom she gave two children. She never wanted children, but when she found out she was pregnant with your babies, that girl was genuinely excited. I fucked up. There's no coming back from what I did to her. I hear she's stealing all my clientele. And now she's on social media, putting my survivors at risk. I deserve all of this."

"Nah, don't do that." Shadow squeezed my thigh. "I'm not off limits. I regret ever fuckin' with their mama," he muttered between his teeth so the little boys wouldn't hear them.

"So, what does this mean? Are we a couple? Do you want to be with me?" I asked, eying the uncomfortable expression on Shadow's face. "I'm not Frankie. I'm not going to fuck with no strings. You were all for fuckin' me when I had a nigga. Now that I'm single and can actually be with you, you're not interested?"

"It's not that simple, and you know it." Shadow leaned back in the chair.

"Why? Because of Rigel?" I exclaimed.

"When did I ever tell you I wanted a relationship?" Shadow calmly asked. "When have you *ever* seen me in a relationship?"

I looked at him, feeling my blood start to boil. "Nigga, what? Who was there for you when your best friend was on that operating table, and one of your residents fucked up on his brain operation? You cried on *my* shoulder! That's how we ended up fuckin' that night! And when I told you that I was pregnant, you looked happy! And when they told you that our little girl was dead, you looked devastated, like a piece of you died with her! Muthafucka, you love every part of me!" I screamed so loud that it caused the little boys to jump.

Shadow's bushy eyebrows connected. "I do. You know I do."

"Yes, we agreed in the past that I wouldn't tell anyone if you wouldn't tell, but everyone knows now! On fuckin' Valentine's Day, you asked me if I was brave enough to date you openly! That you've been wanting to tell everyone for months how I have you feeling! How if I didn't tell Rigel about you soon, that *you* were gonna tell him! Now he knows! Now *everyone* knows! And you have the fuckin' nerve to ask me when did you ever tell me you wanted a relationship? When I started fuckin' you raw, nigga, *that's* when you told me!" I tried to get up from the couch, but the pain in my abdomen pulled me back down.

"I'm not good at this love shit, Bri." Shadow watched me grimace in pain. "I can take care of you physically, but emotionally, I don't even have it together myself. I did some unforgivable shit in my time. I left a son out here to fend for himself, knowing what type of woman Agnes is and what he'd be exposed to. Rigel defended my child support case, watching me fight for my two younger sons. Can you imagine how he must've felt? *You* were about to give birth to his little sister! I killed his mama's new nigga, and I did it in front of her son. Then I went on to live a rich fuckin' life while fuckin' his woman. I'm sorry that you were in so much pain and would have bled to death if you hadn't called 911 when you did. But if my father had done the shit that I did to them, I probably would've done the same thing. You would've been dead, the baby wouldn't have made it as far as it did, and my father would've been executed in front of that medical system that I hadn't reaped the benefits of!"

I looked at him, watching him clench his teeth in anger.

"Asking me if I want a relationship right now is saying fuck what I'm experiencing and fuck what your ex-boyfriend is experiencing. We were wrong. And nah, I didn't give a fuck about fuckin' Rigel's woman when I didn't know he was my own son. But now, at this moment, everything I did to him is sinking in. Give me some time, Brielle. Give yourself some time to get to know your sister again. Maybe she's around the nigga to piss Marley off. Maybe he's the only one she feels was there for her when she needed someone to be there for her. Learn her and give me some time." Shadow got up from the couch. "Your sister's kids are in Maryland with her mother-in-law. One of those babies is a fuckin' rape baby. Fuck a nigga and worry about your family."

I looked up at him as he walked toward the kitchen area of his luxurious open floor plan. I'd never seen that man care about anything other than himself. Learning that his own lawyer was his son was changing him. He wasn't the Shadow that I'd grown to know and love. And it seemed as if he'd never be that person again. I'd lost everything already. I had to do something so I wouldn't lose him as well.

"What are you doing in my daddy's house, hoe?" the two-year-old had the nerve to walk up to me and say, his little brother waddling behind him.

I knew Frankie taught her son that shit.

"That's exactly why y'all daddy has custody of you and your brother." I faked a smile.

I saw then that I was really going to hate the new life that I would have if I stayed in whatever situation I had going on with Shadow. As soon as I was healed, I was going to get my life back on track. I reached in my pocket for my cell phone as the kids got their bad asses the fuck away from me.

How's my sister? I texted Rigel's phone, awaiting a response.

Those three dots jumped up and down, alerting me that Rigel was typing something. Then they stopped. I waited about a minute for him to start texting again. Nothing. So, I texted the muthafucka again.

Can you have Gia give me a call? I texted as fast as I could.

The dots reappeared.

Worry about Shadow, and I'll worry about Gia. When she wants to talk to you, she will. Heal so you won't hurt her. I got her. She's safe with me. Don't text my fuckin' phone looking for her... Rigel had the nerve to text.

Though Rigel was talking for Gia, I was sure her words would've been similar if I was talking to her directly. If I thought my relationship with my sister was a mess before the tragic events over the past two months occurred, things were definitely a mess now that Rigel had come between us. If the twin he had was even Gia.

CHAPTER SEVEN
FRANKIE

"It smells like boiled bacterial vaginosis in this bitch." I plugged my nose, spraying Apple Glade air freshener in the air of the bathroom at my mother's place. My little sister, Sessa, stayed with a fuckin' yeast infection. "Bitch, I told you to stop washing fat ma with that damn Bath and Body Works."

Sessa huffed from her messy ass room. "Frankie, how else am I supposed to keep my pussy smelling like fresh water?"

"It smells more like a swamp in this muthafucka. Girl, book an appointment with my OB-GYN ASAP." I hurried and closed the bathroom door before going to stand in my sister's doorway as she got ready to go to work that night.

Sessa was a traveling stripper. She and her homegirls started this company called Skrippagram, where club owners could book them for nights that featured celebrities. My sister hung around nothing but the baddest bitches. They made Megan Thee Stallion look basic. They all stood five foot nine, ass and thighs for days, face-card never declining, and hair for miles. My sister was the darkest one of her crew, but she wore her complexion like a crown. As dark as she was, she still wasn't as dark as me. Her skin was the color of a brand-new penny, whereas mine was more like coffee without the sugar or the cream.

Mama put all her hopes and dreams into Sessa, the straight-A student. Her youngest daughter, who she always bragged about having brains *and* beauty. Sessa could've been anything she wanted to be, but Mama put a lot of pressure on her, and she couldn't take it. She dropped out of medical school to start her own business, which was actually doing pretty well. She and her crew *each* made over six figures every year. Despite the fact that she basically ran a mobile hoe service, she was still doing better than me in my mother's eyes. I was too dark, too loud, too proud, and too opinionated.

The hate my mother had for me goes way back to Mama catching me in the bed with her boyfriend. I was thirteen years old, and she just knew I had seduced her fuckin' boyfriend. We grew up in the hood, and her boyfriend, Roger, had taken us from the hood and moved us into his place. I'd just started growing breasts, hips, and ass. He probably wanted Sessa, but she was only eight at the time. So, he started touching me and had me doing the same to him until touching wasn't enough. He told me if I told my mother what he was doing to me, he'd throw us out on the street. So, I let him do whatever he wanted. He fucked me for nearly a year before Mama walked in on us. She let the nigga finish. When he was done, he took a shower and went to work. And Mama beat my fuckin' ass. The next day, she left Roger, and we moved in with my aunt, who lived a few blocks from Brielle's grandma.

Brielle knew before I even told her anything that I was being raped. She knew the signs because of the things her grandma had her doing to help pay the bills in her house. Her grandmother died when we were around fifteen. I'd never seen anyone laugh at a funeral, but that's exactly what we did. We both laughed until Brielle started crying. We were all we had those days. My mama made sure not to bring her niggas around me, and she barely ever came to visit my babies once they were born. She was super friendly to Brielle, however, always praising her for being lighter skinned. She was the total opposite of Agnes, who couldn't stand lighter-skinned women. Agnes loved me more than she did Brielle. Anything I needed, she was always there to help. The one thing Agnes and my mama, Uma, had in common was that the bitches loved drama.

Brielle was my best friend. The one person who made me feel safe. The one person who'd beat a bitch's ass if they ever made fun of me for being dark-skinned and overdeveloped at a young age. She was so small and dainty growing up. I was always fetishized by the older boys because of my body. I was so insecure about my body, and she always told me how pretty I was and how I was going to be the baddest bitch when I grew up. She was my sister, my reason to get up in the morning and going to school when my mama didn't even notice a difference in my behavior once Roger started molesting me.

I always felt like Brielle dumbed herself down to be my friend. Like Sessa, Brielle could've been a surgeon, a lawyer, a scientist, anything but a real estate agent. She started that real estate company with me so she wouldn't leave me in Charlotte alone. The girl turned down scholarships to Harvard and UCLA to stay in North Carolina with me, who'd barely gotten into UNC Charlotte.

"You coming with us?" Sessa got up from her bed and went over to grab her bag.

"Girl, you got all this money, and you're still living at home with Mama." I rolled my eyes, watching her go over and throw some clothes in an overnight bag. "Make sure you throw some boric acid suppositories in that bag. You can't swing around that pole upside down with your pussy smelling like that. I'm for real. Pop one of those Azo suppositories up that thang for a minimum of three days. I'm for real. That thang smells angry!"

Sessa huffed in frustration, pushing her long hair from her face. "First of all, I stay with Mama because I pay all her bills. *You* barely come around to cook, clean, or help around here. And second of all," she sighed heavily, "where do I buy the suppositories?"

"At CVS. You need 'em like yesterday. And go to the clinic, sis." I exhaled deeply, folding my arms across my chest. "And coming with y'all where?"

"We got booked at Club Wet on Virginia Beach. Trap Starr is gonna be there, bitch! You down?" Sessa squealed with excitement, clapping her booty cheeks together as she stood in front of her duffle bag. "It's the first of the month, on a Friday, and niggas just got paid. The club owner is talking about giving me twenty thousand for my girls to entertain those niggas all night. You wanna pop out?"

I looked at her. I hadn't seen Brielle since Valentine's Day. Marley had been obsessed with Brielle and Gia for the past two weeks, trying to figure out how to put Gia back in that fuckin' mental institution. Last I heard, Trap's mother had the bitch's kids and wasn't trying to give them back. Not just that, but Gia was somewhere put up with Rigel. I knew Brielle was losing her mind behind that shit, and that should've made me happy, but it didn't. It didn't take away from the fact that she was fuckin' my baby daddy. That he had that fuckin' bitch around my kids. Kids that sometimes I was overwhelmed by taking care of. It wasn't like I had the best example of a mother. My mama was too busy worried about a nigga to raise Sessa or me. And I guess I was following in her footsteps, following behind Shadow's sexy stupid ass.

"How many bitches do you need for this party?" I rolled my eyes playfully as I watched my sister jump up and down, clapping. I shook my head at her, getting a whiff of whatever she had going on between her legs. "Boric acid, asap!"

I'd already planned to go to Virginia Beach that weekend anyway for a showing. I was supposed to be showing three waterfront homes worth $4.5 million that weekend. Might as well make some money along the way. I called up the three agents I'd hired that week. Grammy wanted in on the real estate action. She failed the test three times and finally passed that week. She had a huge internet following and could really put my company on the map. I had her get her real estate license in Virginia so we could sell properties there. Nawi and Chanel were my cousins on my mother's side. They'd only been in America for five years; they just barely got their citizenship and were eager to work for me to make money to send home to their families. All three women were beautiful and would definitely be some eye candy for Trap and his niggas that night.

My sister loaded up about six of her girls and put us on a party bus. We barely made it the five and a half hours to the club in Virginia when that bitch was screaming out in pain that she felt like she was burning between her fuckin' legs. There we were, in a party bus, parked outside of Sentara Virginia Beach General Hospital. Her top paid dancer, Bolivia, went inside with her. After about two hours of sitting outside, pregaming in the bus, Bolivia came out with news that sis had trichomoniasis *and* gonorrhea. They were short a dancer, and guess who they were looking at to fill in for her.

"Sis, I can't go in VIP smelling like the bottom of a fish tank!" Sessa whined to me that night at the hotel we were staying in. The strip club was right on the beach alongside the

Hampton Inn. We went to the hotel to shower and change into sexy attire.

I rolled my eyes, popping my gum. I was *so* not in the mood to dance. I was always that girl who everyone used to draw in the niggas. I may not have been the prettiest bitch, but my body was definitely one of the baddest. That's how I got niggas. It definitely wasn't my personality that reeled them in. It was the fact that I could clap my ass louder than most people could clap their hands. A sexy silhouette reeled the niggas in, but when it came to a pretty face, I would get left every time. So, it shouldn't have shocked me that Shadow chose Brielle.

Sis didn't even give me a chance to say no that night. As soon as she saw me sigh heavily, about to ask her who to talk to at the club, she threw her lanyard containing her company logo around my neck and told me to ask for the club owner, Fat Reggie. Sis stayed behind at the hotel, and I took the girls over to the club. I felt like we were on the slave auction block as the fat nigga lined us up along the hallway, about to split us up and scatter us about the club. I don't know what my sister was thinking to send her girls in that bitch without some sort of security.

Just as I was about to speak up, Grammy yanked on my arm, pointing toward the end of the hallway where Trap and his crew were. I rolled my eyes a little, looking over at the nigga. I wasn't really into light brights, but he *was* fine as hell, dressed in all white, his long, dark curly hair in a man bun on top of his head. There were ten of us in the hallway. He walked down the line, pointing at four along the way until he got to me.

"And this one." He looked me over before looking into my face and licking his lips. "*Definitely* this one."

I pursed my lips, about to say something, when the cocky nigga grabbed me by my wrist, yanking me along with him. I looked back at Grammy, who seemed pissed that he didn't even recognize her, and she'd sung back up for him and written some of the hooks on his songs.

"You know my home girl back there has written music for you, nigga," I spoke over the loud music playing.

"Well, I'm not here to rap or sing, mama. I'm here to see you dance." He looked back at me over his shoulder as the other four girls he picked followed us.

We were led to VIP, where there were even more niggas drooling as we walked through the entire floor upstairs, which overlooked the floor below. The floor above was a club all by itself with three poles for the girls to show his crew what they were working with. I knew he didn't think I was about to climb that shit. I had absolutely no fuckin' body strength. I nodded toward three of the girls to go work their magic on the pole while the fourth girl went over and gave a lap dance to one of the niggas at the bar, who I knew was ballin' by all the jewelry he had on. I exhaled in relief, thinking I was off the hook when Trap pulled my ass over to the couch where he was sitting.

He sat on the leather sofa, pulling me down into his lap. The other girls wasted no time pulling off their skimpy dresses and getting asshole naked. We were already at a damn beach in fuckin' March. They were used to taking it off and busting it wide open for niggas. Shit, I was a real estate agent who was supposed to be up early the next morning to make a sale on a house, not my pussy. That's probably how my sister ended up with two fuckin' sexually transmitted diseases. I looked over at the bar. That nigga was pulling his dick out, and the bitch was already putting her hair up in a ponytail to give the nigga lip service.

I shook my head. "Oh, hell nah." I started to get up from Trap's lap, but he pulled me back down.

"Your homegirls are here to fuck, shawty," Trap whispered,

his lips grazing my shoulder. "Now, unless you want to fuck a few of these niggas, I'd suggest you stay right here on my lap and let these niggas get too drunk to notice when I get you out of here. Ya sister, Sessa, let me keep 10k of the money I was paying her if I didn't let my niggas touch you."

I sighed heavily as he gapped his legs further apart so I could sit between them.

Trap scooted back on the couch, pulling my body further into his. "What do you do, mama? You dance, too?"

I smacked my lips, looking back at him, eying the platinum bottom row of teeth in his mouth. "Nah, I sell real estate. I'm supposed to be up at 9:00 in the morning to show three waterfront properties. So, can you tell your homeboys to hurry up and bust a nut so I can get back to my room and get some sleep?"

I looked around the room at the niggas flicking twenties, fifties, and hundreds at my sister's dancers. They got completely naked for th0se niggas—nothing on but their strip lashes and nail polish. One of the bitches was bent over, with one of the niggas' hands in her pussy and thumb in her ass. Another bitch was letting a nigga snort coke out of her ass crack. The bitch at the bar was gagging on the dick, looking the nigga in his eyes while he gripped the fuck out of her hair. And the last chick was spinning around the pole with a light-up booty plug in her ass, having niggas in a daze. Normally, I would've loved that environment. But I hadn't been myself lately, and my sister's itchy pussy ass felt it, too. She wanted me to get out of town and away from the drama with the bitch who was supposed to be my best friend.

"You wanna get up outta here? Show me one of the properties?" he asked, gripping my waist in his warm hands.

I looked back at him. "Leaving your own party?"

Trap's eyebrows crinkled. "Do these niggas *look* like they'll miss me? Come on, ma. We can leave out the back entrance."

"I just knew you were gonna say, 'Come on, ma, you know I got a wife,' in your Earl Simmons voice." I stood from the couch, and Trap stood behind me. I turned around to face him.

He nodded. "I do have a wife, but she's not here. Mentally and physically. You wanna get out of here or what? My security guards are in this muthafucka. Nothing is gonna happen that your girls don't want to happen."

I spotted his bodyguards standing in every corner of the room like soldiers. One of them was a woman who was looking me dead in the fuckin' face like she wanted to cut my heart out of my chest.

Trap didn't seem to have time for my indecisiveness. He grabbed me by the wrist again, leading me out of VIP, down a hallway toward an exit that led us down some stairs, and out of the club. I'd left my fur coat on the party bus earlier. Luckily, I had taken the keys from my sister before leaving the hotel room, or my ass would've been freezing. Trap waited patiently alongside a black Bugatti Mistral.

"This is what y'all niggas drive when y'all are on tour?" I walked up to him, eyes wide as I looked at the car sparkling under the car lot lights.

"We're on break for about three days. I keep this one parked at my condo, which is about five minutes from the beach." He grinned at me as I ran my fingers over the hood of the car. "You said you were selling houses and shit. I'll buy whatever you're selling."

I looked at him, watching his eyes trace the shape of my hips, the measurements of my waist, and then my breasts. "Listen, Franciska Anita Knowles sells real estate, not pussy."

"If I wanted pussy, I would've had the first turn with any of those females back there at the club," Trap let me know. "You gonna show me one of these properties or nah? I'm selling my house when I get off tour. The kids and I could use a vacation away from every muthafucka. Couldn't you use a break?"

I folded my arms, looking up into his face. "Nigga, let's settle a few things. Do you know who I am? Apparently, you and your crew are familiar with my little sister, but do you know who my old business partner is? I—"

Trap exhaled deeply, moving me out of the way a little so he could open the driver's side door to his ride. The nigga went digging for something in his armrest before coming back with a stack of papers. "Divorce papers, ma. I thought I had my wife back, and she's filing for divorce."

I shrugged, taking the papers in my hand. "Well, maybe you should've brought the bitch on tour with you instead of sending her back to Charlotte to fuck ya friend again."

Trap frowned, crinkling the papers in his hands.

"Your wife's sister was my business partner. Didn't even tell me she had a sister, and I've known her since we were little kids. Your wife doesn't have many screws left in her toolbox, that's for sure. The shit definitely had to be draining. My mother is bipolar. I know all about dealing with bitches with their wires crossed," I told him, watching him shaking his head at the thought of whatever he went through with Gia. "You wanna look at the house, or are we gonna stand out here in this wind and feel sorry for shit we can't do anything about?"

Trap frowned down at me as I snatched those depressing ass papers out of his hand before walking around his fancy car to hop in the passenger side. He hopped in the driver's seat and asked me where we were going. I told him the address to put in the GPS.

In about six minutes, we pulled into the driveway of the beautiful waterfront property. The eight-bedroom house was completely renovated with an outdoor pool, gazebo, kitchen, and pool house. From the look on Trap's face, I don't think he expected the house to be as big as it was.

"I have a mother and two kids. I don't have a wife anymore. What do I need an eight-bedroom house for, mama?" Trap asked as we stood alongside his car, admiring the massive home from the driveway.

"You can have album release parties right here in your house on the beach. You can throw a family reunion and have your family on your mother's side stay in the muthafucka. Shit, you can rent it out as an Airbnb. You can plan your next wedding and let your guests stay here when you get married right over there on the beach before God." I smirked at the irritated expression on Trap's face. "Hey, you're the one who said you wanted to look at one of the $4.5-million-dollar houses that I'm showing tomorrow. You can definitely afford it. You have all this fame and all this fuckin' money, and you're sad over a bitch?"

"I'm sad over fuckin' time spent, time lost, time I'll never get the fuck back. I've known her for twelve years and never knew she had a sister—nah, *sisters,* plural—until a few weeks ago!" Trap exclaimed. "I've protected her name. I've protected her kids, *our* kids. I tried getting her the help she needed before she killed herself or our son. She gets pregnant by her own perverted-ass fuckin' father, and I have my mother believing the baby is mine, so she'll help the girl take care of her! Gia is out free when she needs help that she can't get out here on the streets. And instead of letting me help her, she's divorcing me. And guess who her lawyer is? The same nigga I paid to help me find her when she escaped that mental institution." He laughed to himself as he watched me pull a blunt I'd rolled up earlier from my purse.

"I'm so sick of those hoes," I muttered. "I've known Brielle practically all my life and didn't know about her sisters either, love. Apparently, they're part of a life Brielle wanted to forget. A past that should've stayed where the fuck they were. Gia has Marley obsessing over how she got out of that facility. Gia was fuckin' on Knight, and—" I laughed a little as Trap snatched my blunt and my sparkly lighter from my hands.

"We both fucked other muthafuckas. I'm not pressed over that shit." Trap lied to himself because he definitely wasn't lying to me. He put the blunt to his lips and lit it, inhaling deeply, holding in the vapors before exhaling slowly. "Me and Knight were both preacher's kids. That's how I know the nigga. His father had what they called dissociative identity disorder. His mama took her kids one day and left him. The nigga has seen some shit in his time. Makes sense that he became a doctor, trying to understand the shit. Makes even more sense why he took an interest in Gia. He ended up taking the fall for me on a drug charge when we were teens. Ended up at the group home where he met Gia. He asked me how to approach her and tell her how he felt. When I ended up at the same group home, I showed the nigga how to talk to her. So, I guess all this shit that's happening is my karma."

I wasn't even sure what to say to the nigga. I just wanted to sell houses. I expected to meet a nigga who was just there to party, not someone who wanted to vent. Trap left a club full of hoes to go look at a house on the beach. He left his entourage, left security, and wanted to be alone with me, the sister of the woman who supplied the girls for the celebrity's entire crew to do whatever they wanted with them.

"Gotta move on, buddy." I took my blunt from his hand and took a few hits.

"You've never been in love? Never been married?" Trap asked. "I don't know how old you are, but a nigga will be thirty in three fuckin' years. I'm retiring from rap by the time I'm thirty-five. I'm just gonna produce, write music, and build for my family. I'm not gonna be that nigga in the club with his crew, fuckin' bitches in VIP. After all that fuckin' and gettin' sucked on, you wake up the next morning, not even remembering the face of the bitch who was suckin' your dick or letting you fuck her and her friend. I don't remember any of their faces. The only face I remember when it's said and done is the face of the woman who I threw in a mental institution to stop her from ending it all."

"Did I mention there's a jacuzzi tub in the master bedroom, which is on the first floor?" I changed the subject.

Trap frowned at my lack of ability to let him get me down that night. "A nigga can't vent?"

I shook my head, exhaling smoke from my nose. "I don't wanna hear this shit. I guarantee you that Gia is not fuckin' crying over you. And if she *is* crying, I'm sure she's somewhere crying on another nigga's dick. And it's probably not even Knight's dick! Nah, Gia isn't in her right mind, but even she's not gonna wanna share a nigga with his wife for too long. Especially not the wife who knew her sister was carrying around a dead baby in her uterus for a few days."

The first time Mama made her famous tea was when I told her I was pregnant a few weeks after she left her boyfriend. She made me sit and watch as she prepared the tea from herbs in her sister's garden. It only took a few hours for the tea to make me cramp violently. She took me to the hospital that night, watching me crying in pain as the surgeons had to perform a D&C to get rid of the rest of the birth material that hadn't passed through me. In a person as far along as Brielle was, the tea wouldn't actually kill a baby instantly. It would only cause the placenta to separate from the uterine wall, causing massive bleeding. Once the bleeding started, you'd need to hurry to the hospital, or you'd bleed to death, or the baby could suffocate.

I'd played a part in Brielle's pain, and for that, I did feel some type of way. I didn't want to kill the bitch; I just wanted her to feel the agony that I felt when I figured out that she was fuckin' Shadow. *My* Shadow. The man who I'd loved for the past three years that I'd known him. One baby after the next, and he still didn't love me. And I couldn't figure out why until I discovered that it was because he loved Brielle. My best friend, my everything. The bitch I'd cry to *about* the nigga! I was crying about missing the dick, and she was fuckin' the nigga behind my back. Yeah, I was hurting, but did I want to talk about it with Trap, her sister's husband? Nah, I didn't wanna fuckin' talk.

"I'm sick of this fame shit. I gotta get my staff drunk just so I can move around alone. The club owner made sure no one knew our location. By the time word is out that I'm at the club, I'm out here with you. If you don't wanna talk about problems, cool." Trap finally agreed to stop talking about depressing shit.

I nodded, sighing in relief. "Can we take a look around? If you're not gonna put in a bid for the house, I can at least use this time as practice for what I'm gonna say to the other six billionaires who are coming through tomorrow to take a look around." I turned and walked toward the porch steps.

Trap followed close behind, his cologne floating in the air around me. His smell was intoxicating, and I guess mine was to him as well. "What's that smell you're wearing?" he asked as I entered the code on the padlock and checked my phone for the passcode to deactivate the alarm once we were inside.

"Wild Rose Coach." I grinned a little over my shoulder. "I have on a fur coat, and you can still smell it? Damn."

"Shit smells good as fuck," Trap commented, close behind me as we entered the home and the alarm sounded.

I hurried toward the console to cut off the alarm as it started beeping.

"Yeah, this shit is lit." Trap walked into the house, admiring the open layout.

"Hell yeah," I responded as I pressed the code to deactivate the system. "This is the life right here. Parties, family, kids, vacation, straight luxury living." I turned around to face him, watching him walk toward the living/dining area.

Trap stopped at the sliding door and gazed out at the waves crashing against the shore. "Man, I bet this is the best sound to wake up to in the morning. Nothing but waves and wind. Seagulls and shit."

"A forty-three-year-old woman whose ex-husband owns half the damn television networks in the US won this house in a settlement," I let him know. I walked into the furnished living room, eying a fancy sound system that was mounted over the fireplace. I picked up the remote that was next to it. "This is some sophisticated '80s baby shit. I see Mama still had CDs and shit." I laughed to myself as I powered the system on.

As soon as it came on, Mary J. Blige's song, "Not Gon' Cry," blasted through the entire house.

Trap looked back at me, and we both burst out laughing.

I threw my hands in the air, singing along, "While all the time that I was loving you, you were busy loving yourself... bitch-ass nigga." Had to throw that on at the end.

"Lil mama was in her feelings. Got damn." Trap chuckled as I turned the system down a little.

"Muthafucka, I would stop breathing if you told me to, and now you're busy loving some other bitch." I sang my own words to the song as I walked over to the refrigerator, where I made sure the seller put a few bottles of wine for whoever bought her depressing ass house.

"Shit, sounds like you've got some shit to get off your chest, too," Trap noticed.

"Yeah, this house, so I can get this commission." I rolled my eyes, grabbing a bottle of Armand de Brignac Rose champagne. I reached into the cabinet for two polished wine bottles.

"Besides the kids, I have nothing to show..." I heard Trap sing to himself.

I smiled a little before my smile faded, realizing I didn't have shit to show but two kids either. Two kids who I no longer had full custody of. I had to visit my own kids on weekends, and the visit had to be fuckin' supervised. I opened one of the drawers and grabbed a corkscrew so I could pop the cork on the bottle. I imagined myself gouging Brielle's eyes out with the bottle opener as I stabbed the cork, driving the corkscrew into it.

Trap stepped out of his white mid-top Christian Louboutin leather sneakers, leaving them by the throw rug in front of the sliding door. I popped the cork out of the bottle and watched it fizzle a little before pouring us both a glass. I pulled off my coat, draping it across the back of one of the bar stools. Then I grabbed the glasses and brought them over to where Trap stood, watching the waves.

Trap turned to me as I approached him and handed him a glass. He grinned, watching me drink half of my glass before lowering it.

"Well, come on, let me show you around." I rolled my eyes at the nigga looking me over in the skimpy dress that my sister had me wearing. No bra and thong panties that were uncomfortable as fuck, stuck up my ass.

It took me a good thirty or forty-five minutes to show that man the entire property. I loved everything about that place. I wished I could live in luxury. As much as my mama hated me, I'd still move the bitch into the house. Maybe hire a nurse or two to take care of her. I'd move my sister in, so I could watch over her. I'd turn one of the rooms into an office space. Another into a gym. Another into a library with a window seat so I could listen to the rain while I read books by my favorite urban fiction author, Krystal Armstead. That bitch will have you ready to throw your kindle and shit. Petty bitch, but I loved her, though.

Oh, then I'd have a playroom for the kids. That master bathroom was to fuckin' die for. I'd spend hours in that marble shower or soak until my skin was wrinkled in that hot tub. The double sink was wide enough so my future nigga could keep his shit on his side and not worry about my flat iron that I always forgot to unplug.

"Yeah, this is the life right here," Trap told me as we ended up back in the kitchen, pouring another glass of champagne after we completed the tour. He eyed the missing knobs on the stove. "What's up with the stainless-steel knobs missing?"

"Oh," I responded after taking a quick sip from the glass. "The seller said after she broke up with her husband, he took all the food out of the fridge, the knobs off the stove, the wifi out of his name, batteries out of all of the remotes, bills out of his name, everything he bought had to fuckin' go."

"Nigga petty." Trap chuckled before taking a few sips.

"She just put new appliances in this muthafucka. I'll remind her about the knobs for this beautiful Bosch stove. This is my fuckin' dream house." I looked around the kitchen.

"You deserve to live your dreams." Trap grabbed the bottle and nodded toward the sliding door.

"Only in my dreams will I live like this." I was real with myself as I followed Trap toward the door.

He opened the door, and we stepped outside, closing the door behind us.

The lights that surrounded the pool made the pool a deep blue, just like the ocean, which wasn't too far from the house. As windy as it was, that damn liquor had me feeling comfortably warm. Back at the club, there was a food truck selling wings and shit. Trap called to check on his crew and my sister's girls, then asked that female bodyguard if she could bring twenty ranch wings from the food truck. About thirty minutes later, the bodyguard showed up with the wings.

She rolled her eyes hard as fuck after handing the bag to Trap. "Jefe, you want me to stay and keep watch?" she asked him.

"Nah, we're good," Trap tried telling her.

"I'll be standing out front." She looked at me sideways before leaving us on the patio and walking through the house to wait out front.

"The fuck is wrong with her?" I watched her walk away.

Trap shook his head, setting the bag on the umbrella table. He barely got the styrofoam tray out of the bag when the aroma of those freshly fried wings started floating through the air. I didn't know what it was, but there was nothing better than eating chicken wings with your eyes closed, drunk as fuck.

We sat at that table, drunk as fuck, eating the meat completely off the bone of all twenty wings in that styrofoam. I'd turned the music up earlier. The seller had speakers in every room of the house, including her backyard. I was twerking in my seat as soon as Drake and 21 Savage's "Hours in Silence" flowed through the speakers.

"Aye," I closed my eyes, bending over in my seat, twerking one cheek at a time.

"So, why are you single?" Trap asked, about to fuck up my buzz.

I opened my eyes and glared at him as he handed me the last chicken wing. I snatched it from him. "You lucky you gave me the last wing, or you would've gotten cursed out right then. Why you gotta ask stupid shit like that? The question *should* be, why don't niggas want girls like me? I know I have some shit to work on, but damn. There are niggas out here in love with women at the nut house, and I can't even get a nigga to text back! No offense, but it's real."

"None taken. It's not your fault niggas chose the wrong ones. Maybe you surround yourself with the wrong niggas," Trap commented, watching me chew into the chicken wing. "Gotta find another life to live."

"I dated hood niggas. I've dated *good* niggas. I've dated broke niggas. I've dated rich niggas. I've dated old niggas. I've dated young niggas. I've dated black niggas. I've dated *white* niggas! I've dated this nigga, I've dated *that* nigga. I'm *over* niggas." I ate the meat down to the bone, even the grizzle. I sucked the bone dry before tossing it into the tray.

Tray eyed my lips. "If you suck a nigga's meat off the bone like you did that piece of chicken, I know they were losing their minds."

I shook my head. "You know sex doesn't keep nann nigga. For a little while, it'll have his head gone, but if that's all we have, then both of us will eventually move on. I used to think that if I did every magic trick in my bag to a nigga, he'd stick around forever. Now, I'm watching my nigga raise *my* kids with another bitch. The nigga I thought I had was fuckin' my best friend, had *her* nigga defending him in court for custody, and he *won*! I'm far from the perfect mother, but I didn't deserve that shit."

"Shit, the nigga who's my private investigator and was supposed to be keeping an eye on Gia is now *her* divorce attorney. Rigel Worth." Trap watched me look at him with my eyes as wide as I could get them.

"Yeah, that's Brielle's ex-nigga, and my ex-nigga's lawyer." I shook my head, eying the empty bottle of champagne. I pushed my bangs from my face. "You got me out here in my feelings, drunk as fuck. I didn't wanna talk about this shit."

The wind was blowing so hard that hair flew in the corner of my mouth.

Trap reached for my face, pulling my hair from my lips. "Maybe we need to take this nigga out."

I laughed a little, pushing his hand from my face. "You must not know this nigga's family. He's surrounded by nothing but dirty rich niggas. They will kill you, and no one will ever find your fuckin' body. I heard he even had homeless niggas watching his back. He has a nigga on every corner watching his back. He might be alone, but he's never alone, if you know what I mean. You gotta be a slick muthafucka to catch him slippin'. So don't think you'll ever run up on him and make it out of that situation alive. Surprised Brielle made it out alive. Now, *she's* the one who needs to count her blessings. I just want to leave the world behind and forget these muthafuckas."

"Wanna fly out to Napa Valley? You ever been on the wine train?" Trap asked.

I just looked at him like he couldn't have been talking to me.

"For real?" He frowned, scooting his chair from the table. "Let's catch a flight, turn the phones off, and vibe out."

I wasn't even sure what to say. "I have a real estate company to run."

"And? I have a tour to go on." Trap clicked his teeth. "You said you wanted to get away. You need to. I do, too, at least for a few days. We can go anywhere you wanna go and be back by Tuesday night. I promise you, once we go to this shit, you'll want me to fly you out again."

I shook my head at him. "I have a showing tomorrow morning."

Trap nodded. "Show all five clients all three places at the same time. Let them put their bids in and let me know what they're bidding for this place, so a nigga can bid higher. Whatever commission you earn for the house, I'll double it."

I exhaled deeply, not quite sure about his ass. "This is the liquor talkin', nigga."

"Maybe. But we need to shut the world out, even if it's only temporary," Trap tried to convince me.

"This is crazy." I was in disbelief of how Gia could toss his ass to the curb. I didn't understand. "No way a nigga is this perfect. You must ain't got no dick. Light skin niggas too pretty. No way you have looks *and* dick."

Trap laughed a little. "I'll show you mine if you show me yours." He reached for my chair, pulling it closer to his.

The way he pulled all 165 pounds of me toward him sent my hormones soaring. Not just that, but he didn't even give me a chance to deny him access to see some skin. He reached up my dress to hook his fingers around the elastic of my panties.

I giggled a little, lifting my booty so he could pull my panties from my body.

The fool smelled them before tossing them on the table. "Your pussy smells like fuckin' syrup. Is that how she tastes, too?" he asked me before standing from his chair.

I looked up at his face before looking down at him, lifting his shirt around his rippled chest. The nigga's body was fuckin' perfect. As he moved closer to me, I reached for his chest to run my hands across his chiseled body. I watched as he unzipped his pants, revealing his burgundy boxers. The bulge in his boxers spoke for itself. I gulped at the sight of the bulge, wishing I could take back the words I'd just said a few seconds earlier.

"Reach in and grab it." He bit his lip, looking down at me.

When I hesitated, he grabbed my hand and placed it inside his boxers.

As soon as I grabbed his dick, it grew in my hands. I didn't have to pull it out to know it had to be the biggest dick I'd ever seen. I pulled it through the hole in his boxers and stared it in the eye. That thang was so pretty. So pretty that it could've been a dildo model. He had one of those dicks that I knew whatever bitch he fucked wished it was detachable. He didn't need to go anywhere with her dick. And I was holding it in my hand, *both* hands, and I still wasn't covering the whole thing.

"Now, *who* doesn't have a dick?" Trap asked.

"Who would say such a thing?" I laughed nervously.

"It's in your face. What you gonna do with him?" Trap placed his hands over mine, leading his dick to my lips.

I slipped my hands from under his, sticking out my tongue as I let him slide his dick through my lips. I looked up at him, not flinching or gagging as he slid his dick as far as my throat muscles would allow him to go.

"Got damnnnnn." He looked down at me, watching the saliva flow from the corners of my lips.

I gripped his thighs in my hands, pulling him even further into my mouth. He couldn't do shit but grab my hair. If I wasn't good at anything else, I was good at making a nigga feel at home in my mouth. The way this nigga touched me was different. He ran his fingers through my fuckin' hair, massaging my scalp. That shit made my throat relax around his dick. Before I knew it, my lips were touching the base of his dick, tongue sliding between his balls.

Trap had my hair in a ponytail at that point, standing on his tiptoes. He gripped my hair with one hand and gripped the table with his other hand. He was trying his best not to tremble as I started to bob up and down on his dick. I looked up at him the entire time. Every time he attempted to look away, I gripped his thighs tighter, pulling him closer and deeper down my throat. Saliva was dripping from my chin and his thighs as I sped up the pace. I wanted to taste his kids in my mouth.

It never took me long to make a nigga bust in my mouth. I loved giving head first to see how much stamina a nigga actually had. Most niggas were through after I put that Gawk Gawk 3000 on them. I just knew he was done once he squirted down my throat. I sucked until the last drop and kept on sucking until he was hard again.

I had the nigga laughing, pulling his dick from my mouth. I grinned up at him, licking my lips. The nigga slid his hands around my neck as I stood from the chair. And he pulled my face to his, suckin' my lips into his mouth. That shit felt so good. Just as he turned me around to face the table, Webbie's "Give Me That" blew through the speakers.

We both laughed a little, both singing along, "You know you want it, girl. Don't act like you don't want it. Girl, you want it just as bad as I do…"

"Yo Big Seller has one hell of a playlist. Mood swings like a muthafucka throughout that divorce." Trap pushed my dress over my hips.

I giggled, looking back at him as he tilted his head quizzically to get a good view of my ass. I knew my pussy was smiling back at him. I arched my back, making my ass clap. I knew my pussy was dripping wet. Something about suckin' dick always made my pussy leak. And I'd never sucked a dick that big before.

"Your dick tastes so good. That bitch—*all* them bitches—are crazy," I told him.

Trap held his dick, tapping it on my ass cheeks, watching them clap together. "Clap them cheeks on this fuckin' dick then," he growled, watching me hold my cheeks open so he could slide in. "Sexy chocolate muthafucka. Grab the fuckin' table, and don't fuckin' run."

I don't know why I loved the sound of that shit. My toxic trait was I always loved to fuck around and find out. My favorite words to hear from a nigga were, "What happened to all that shit you was talkin'?", "Move your fuckin' hand," and "Bitch, you better not run." Whew, I'd pick arguments just to hear a nigga say that shit.

Trap wasn't your usual celebrity. I'd been around enough to know how bougie and entitled they were. Have you ever been to a fuckin' Trap Starr concert? That muthafucka's VIP tickets cost $4000-$5000. You gotta pay to play with that muthafucka, and he was on a damn beach with *me*. That nigga just wanted to vent and be around someone he could relate to. He wanted love; I could feel that shit. I wasn't his girl, but damn if he didn't fuck me like I was that night outside on that patio that I wasn't even supposed to be on.

I stretched my arms over my head, gripping the umbrella table, lying flat on my stomach. And he rested his weight on mine for a few seconds. He kissed my shoulders, my neck, my ears. His hands intertwined with mine as he sank into me. His dick filled me up. The shit hurt so good. It had been nearly three months since I'd been with anyone. My friends swore I was a fuckin' hoe. And Brielle swore Shadow was only fuckin' her. The nigga was in my bed the week before he flew that other bitch out to Texas. I was sick of only being sex to a nigga. I needed to mean more to someone. I needed to be a better mother. I needed to be a better me.

Everything I was feeling at that moment turned into real tears rolling down my face. And Trap heard my whimpers. "You good?" he asked, slowing down his strokes.

"I just wanna..." I whimpered. "I just wanna mean something. Anything. I'm somebody, too."

Trap ran his fingers through my hair, kissing my neck. "We can mean something to each other right now. I can get sex any fuckin' where. You're not just sex. Wipe those fuckin' tears and toot that ass up for me."

I sniffled, wiping my face, propping myself up on my elbows as he stood back up straight and slid one hand around my neck. I sighed heavily as he released his hand from my neck. He lifted my right leg, bending it at the knee and pushing it up onto the table. My eyes immediately crossed as he started to plow into me. And when I say plow, I mean that shit. He dug into me with every intention of making me feel every inch, vein, artery, and capillary in that thang he toted between his legs. That thing was so smooth and amazing. He fucked me so good, my pussy was beat-boxing. He pumped my pussy to the beat of the song. It always felt like we were dancing the freakiest dance.

His hands gripped my waist, his thumbs pressing into the small of my back. Then, my song, "Hotbox" by Ne-Yo and Eric Bellinger, had to start playing. I started grinding back, and he knew the words, too. Oh, my mind was gone.

"I needed this shit," I had to tell him. I looked back at him, watching him eying his dick going in and out of me.

"I needed this shit, too. That pussy is talking to a nigga, got damn." He moaned. "Can I put it in your ass?"

My eyes widened. Of all the freaky shit I'd ever done, I'd never let a nigga in my bootyhole. I bit my lip, unsure how to respond. I just tooted my ass in the air, and he took that as a yes.

He spit a huge glob of saliva into the crack of my ass before he took his right hand and grabbed it. He slid his thumb into my bootyhole to train it a little. That wasn't so bad; it felt really good, actually. But I wasn't prepared for that big dick of his to enter my body. I shouted out in pain as he slid that muthafucka in just about an inch or two.

"Noooo!" I whined when he put all his weight on me, causing his dick to go a little further.

The shit hurt but felt good at the same time. Kind of like when you have to take a shit and can't get it out. The shit gives a sort of satisfaction when it passes through, but it hurts if it's a hard poop. Know what I mean? Maybe it's just for me, but the fullness of shit passing through my rectum feels satisfying.

"You said you wouldn't fuckin' run. Remember?" he reminded me, kissing my neck.

"I know, but, shit, muthafucka, got *damn!*" I yelped. The muthafucka laughed in my fuckin' ear. "Easy, oh!"

Trap slid his hand over my stomach and between my legs.

I lifted my pelvis from the table, giving him room to play with my clit and causing him to go deeper inside my rectum.

"Ssshhh, relax, baby." He tried to ease my pain as he rubbed my clit.

And he kept rubbing her until my pussy started talking to him again, then he started pumping inside of me again. My asshole started to relax, and he sank inside, going past the first hump and then the second. Before I knew it, the nigga was balls deep. His balls clapped against my ass as he pumped inside me until we came together.

I panted as he pulled out of me, smacking my ass cheeks. "Oh, what a fuckin' night..." I sighed loudly, looking back at him as he stumbled back.

"Now, go pack your shit so we can take that flight tomorrow, mama." He winked at me.

CHAPTER EIGHT
LONDYN

I'd been in Charlotte going on three weeks, and I'd yet to see Brielle. Rigel had in his mind that it was best that I stay the fuck away from her. He didn't trust anyone, especially not anyone who was involved with the Shades. The month of March was almost gone, and Rigel spent most of his time working on cases and digging up dirt on my foster family and the family that I was married into. The fact that he had friends in high places really had a hand in him not being taken in for Matthew being killed. It didn't hurt that the security guard he had vouching for him died at the hospital from his wounds. The fact that he confirmed what happened in that room before he died helped Rigel get away with what happened.

On top of trying to gather evidence to reopen my case, he was trying to help Gia get custody of her kids. He couldn't get up with Trap. The nigga had him on his block list. And when Rigel tried texting from other phones, he found out the nigga had his shit on do not disturb, and so did his bitch ass mama, Katrina. Rigel was trying to do shit the legal way but fuck that.

My entire reason for switching places with my sister was to help fix her life as much as I could. I'd already fucked up by fuckin' her husband; shit, I needed that shit at the time.

I stayed away from Knight, who she had no business fuckin' around with in the first place. He needed to figure things out with his wife, who seemed to be just as lost and confused as he was. Marley was going to cause problems; I could feel that shit. I had to figure out a way to get my sister's kids back before that bitch figured out that I wasn't Gia. I still had Carmen's number. It didn't take me five minutes to convince her to help me track down Katrina to get my niece and nephew. For whatever reason, even though she worked for Trap, she was loyal to me. Like she knew some shit about Trap that she couldn't tell me. He was the nigga paying her, so she could only tell me so much.

I sat on Rigel's back porch, eyeing the concrete slab across the pond where my house was being built. I smiled at the fact of someone finally taking me out of survival mode. I'd been a part of rich families as far as I could remember, but money couldn't buy me the freedom I needed. Mentally, I was still that scared little girl hiding from my foster uncles. I never had anything that was completely mine. Yeah, my mother-in-law left me money that I'd never be able to touch. If it wasn't for Gia letting me switch places with her, I'd never be able to touch that money.

I never knew what it was like to breathe without someone telling me how I was supposed to walk, talk, smell, and interact. I could wake up and do nothing if I wanted. I could take a shower without someone coming into the bathroom and expecting sex. I could eat what I wanted without someone telling me what I could and couldn't eat. My body was mine to do as I wanted, with whom I wished. It had been a month to the day since Rigel had come back into my life, and he'd yet to touch me in any way that wasn't completely platonic.

The week before, my period came on. I hadn't had a period since before I was sexually assaulted by my ex-husband's family. I was told my ovaries weren't releasing eggs anymore and that I'd never have another period. And there I was, the week before, sitting on the toilet, bleeding. I'd screamed, waking Rigel up from his sleep. I told him to run to the 24-hour CVS and get me a pack of Always with Wings. That nigga came back with Always super pads and buffalo wings from 7-11. When he shot my father and his goons, I knew then that he was that nigga. But coming back with food and a band-aid for my pussy, he could have whatever he wanted from me.

Tired of waiting for Brielle to get out of whoever's bed she was in, I decided to make a move on my own to see her. Rigel wasn't home, so I went into his office and dug through his mail. After searching through his mail—which the OCD nigga had in alphabetical order—I found an invitation addressed to them both. It looked like an invitation to some business banquet. The mail was dated a few months ago, which let me know that either they didn't go or they didn't go together. That nigga worked 24/7, and according to Gia, Brielle worked long hours as well. Still, the invitation was addressed to them both at an address that definitely wasn't the one I was staying at with Rigel. I assumed it was her address.

I showered and changed into a cropped hoodie and high-waisted leggings, an outfit I'd picked out of the shit Brielle had at Rigel's place. I had to jump into those leggings, but I got them on. Sis had some little ass feet. The only shoes in the closet that I could fit were her Crocs. I got dressed and used Rigel's house phone to call a cab. He'd bought me an iPhone 15 Pro Max, and I barely knew what that shit was. When I was committed in 2014, the iPhone 5 was out. I was only allowed to accept calls and not make any in those days. An iPhone didn't mean shit to me, but it was how Rigel kept in touch. I didn't want him tracking me to Brielle's place. The first thing he did when he activated the phone was share locations with each other. I left the phone on his desk and was out the door as soon as the cab showed up.

The cab pulled up to Brielle's place, and I couldn't help but hum, "Looked at my kingdom, I was finally there. To sit on my throne as the prince of Bel Air."

The cab driver looked back at me and grinned. "Doesn't look like anyone's home. You want me to take you back home?"

I looked at him before looking back at Brielle's white house with the white picket fence. I shook my head. "Nah, I'm good." I opened the car door and got out, closing it behind me.

The cab driver didn't leave immediately. He watched me walk up to the porch and ring the doorbell. I eyed the doorbell camera as I hit the doorbell a few times. I huffed, about to turn around and walk up to the cab, when a black SRT Dodge Charger pulled into the driveway, blocking the cab in. The driver's side door opened, and Knight's tall, dark, and sexy ass emerged.

I shook my head, preparing myself to hear his bullshit. We barely talked at the hospital other than the nigga telling me who Rigel was and why I should stay away from him. I was so high that day, and he was going in on how I needed to stay the fuck away from Rigel. He pulled up on me like he was waiting on a bitch to show up at my sister's place sooner or later.

"She's not here. She's in Lexington with my brother." Knight walked up the sideway.

I eyed him before looking back at his car. I wasn't stupid. I knew he had niggas with him. I looked back at him. "What's up?" I asked.

Knight approached the porch and stood at the bottom of

the stairs. "'What's up?'" He looked at me like I had him totally fucked up. "You've been fuckin' that nigga?"

"Nigga, have you been fuckin' your wife? The fuck kind of question is that?" I asked, folding my arms.

I don't know what he had going on with Gia, but the shit wasn't happening with me. Neither he nor Trap even realized I wasn't Gia. I could excuse Trap a little for not really knowing the difference; it had been a year since he'd seen Gia. But Knight was just fuckin' the bitch a month ago, and he couldn't see that I wasn't her? Nah, fuck him.

Knight looked me over a little before looking into my face. "He's trouble."

"And so are you. You're married to my fuckin' psychiatrist. Do you know she went to The Bayou, trying to get my records?" I stepped down to where he was, standing before him. "I talked to the psychiatrist there. She said she took Brielle with her to try to get access to visit my twin, too! The bitch tries to get me thrown away for life, then wants to play nice with my sister to dig up more dirt? And you're worried about Rigel? He was doing his job by turning me in. Marley was trying to hurt not just me but my fuckin' sister. If I were you, I'd be concerned for *her* safety, not mine."

"You really wanna play this game with me? I lost you to my homeboy years ago. I'll be damned if I lose you to a nigga I just found out is my nephew. The same nephew who's fuckin' my wife!" Knight exclaimed. "The nigga's mama could've killed your sister by giving her that tea. The nigga used my wife to get to you. The nigga bought a ring for your sister three months ago!"

I just stared at him blankly.

Knight laughed a little. "You got me fucked up, Gia."

"Nah, *you* and your brother have *Rigel* fucked up. How would you feel if your own father was fuckin' your girl? How would you feel if you stared your father in the face, defended him in court, won custody of the nigga's kids, and he *still* didn't realize he was your fuckin' father?" I shoved Knight in his chest.

"He's used Brielle to piss off my brother, and he's using you to get to me, and you don't see that! I don't have shit to do with whatever the fuck Shadow did to him or his mother. And my mother didn't have shit to do with whatever Shadow did to her! I found out that Agnes is the reason my mother is gone. She's the reason my mother's face was blown out in front of me! Rigel is probably angry at a nigga because I don't remember him either, but I don't remember *shit* before that day my mother's brains were splattered all over IHOP!" Knight yelled at me.

I shook my head. "You're too late, Knight. We had our chance nine years ago. It's over with Trap. He threw me in that place when I needed him. I know it was for my own safety, but I felt abandoned, a feeling I've battled my entire life. Then, here you come, married as fuck to my old roommate. She's been in love with you since before you and I even met. Give *her* a chance. *She's* the one you should put all your effort into." I remembered the words my sister told me that he'd said to her when she called his wife a bitch. "You told me that you'd die behind her, and *I'd* die behind her, too. What happened to all that energy? Huh?"

Knight looked like I'd just ripped his heart from his chest. "I couldn't love her because I was too busy in love with you. She was there when you weren't; she was my best friend when you left me. She would've never fucked Rigel if I had never fucked with you. You left me, and she stayed. And I risked everything I have just for you to tell me that I'm too fuckin' late? Then who's on time? Rigel? You really think I'm gonna just let you be with the nigga whose family slaughtered mine?"

"Do you really think I'd let you anywhere near the nigga who saved me from my father?" I growled back.

Knight's glare was venomous, and then he started laughing like he couldn't believe the words that came out of my mouth. "So, this is where it ends, huh?"

"Nah, this is where I start," I let him know. "You and your niggas can back up so the cab driver can leave. And if you think you're gonna follow me, I promise I'll have something waiting wherever you pull up. I'm not the Gia I was before your wife turned me in. I'm on my meds, and my mind is clear."

Knight's eyebrows knitted together for a second or two before they loosened, and he backed away from me. "You know I still have that necklace you bought me for my eighteenth birthday. I'm still wearing this shit." He started to unhook it from around his neck.

"Keep it. You've worn it this long. I'm sure you've fucked Marley with that chain on. I want no parts of that shit." I huffed.

Knight grinned a little. "You want out of my bed and out of my head, huh? Just act as though the past few months didn't happen, right?"

"Never happened," I agreed. "I shouldn't have wanted anything that belonged to someone else. Go back to your wife. She's got pussy, too, nigga."

Knight nodded. "Bet." He grinned before turning around and walking back to his car.

I walked toward the cab driver as Knight pulled out of the driveway and sped off down the street. I got back into the cab, closing the door behind me.

"Was that Dr. Knight Shade?" The cab driver watched Knight drive off in his rearview mirror.

"Unfortunately." I rolled my eyes, heart pounding in my chest as his final words echoed in my head. I knew exactly what that nigga meant by 'bet.' In Knight's mind, I had just waged war, and the cab driver felt it, too.

"Wherever he went, he's getting back up." The driver exhaled.

"Don't I know it?" I whispered to myself.

"Why did you even go to Brielle's place?" Jaliyah exclaimed over the phone that night. "From what Gia tells me, Knight doesn't play about her. And something tells me that it won't take him long to realize you're not Gia. You were drugged and in a hospital gown the last time he saw you a few weeks ago. You're out and about now, probably looking pretty and in your right frame of mind. You and Gia are identical, but anyone who knows you both will know something is off. You said Rigel knew you weren't Gia the first day he ran into you. Knight will figure it out, and his wife is trying to figure the shit out herself."

I sighed, listening to Jaliyah go off on me on speaker.

The moment Rigel found out about my love for art, he cleared out one of his rooms and turned it into an art studio for me while I stayed with him. He bought me canvas, drawing paper, brushes, oil paint, acrylic paint, watercolor paint, chalk, crayons, colored pencils, drawing pencils, and easels. I was living an artist's dream, and I wasn't going to let Jaliyah's common sense ruin that.

I was in the middle of creating a body impression masterpiece. I'd painted two 36x48-sized canvases black with acrylic paint before spreading red acrylic paint all over my body. I'd just imprinted my breasts, torso, and knees onto one and my ass, thighs, and hands onto another. I was on my hands and knees, about to fill in the spots that didn't imprint the way I wanted them to, when I heard the alarm chime and the front door open down the hall.

"Jaliyah, baby, I have to go," I told her.

"I'm coming to visit you on Saturday, bitch," Jaliyah warned me. "Be safe, and I'll keep Gia safe."

We both made smooching noises before she pressed end on her phone. I exhaled deeply, knowing Rigel was aware that I'd run into his uncle while sneaking off to Brielle's house. I felt Rigel in the doorway before I looked up to see him standing there in his suit and tie. Man, that nigga was fine.

"I covered up my wound, which is healing, by the way." I showed him that I'd wrapped my arm with Saran Wrap.

Rigel set his briefcase alongside the door. His thick eyebrows crinkled as he leaned against the wall, eyeing me completely naked on my knees, covered in paint. My hair was up in a bun to stay out of my way.

"Trap may not have noticed you switched with your sister, but it won't take Knight long to figure that shit out."

"Look now, don't start with me. I ain't in the mood today, Ike." I huffed. "I wanted to see Brielle, okay? Had no idea Knight was lurking in the area. You know the nigga pulled up on me, talking about some necklace I'd given him when he was eighteen."

"Eighteen?" Rigel made a face. "From what I researched on your sister, she left Wake Hills at sixteen and married Trap at eighteen. Gia lost contact with Knight way before either turned eighteen."

I cringed, realizing the nigga was baiting me. Marley probably talked the nigga into staking out my sister's place, hoping I'd eventually show up to look for her. I looked up at Rigel, who was already taking off his jacket to calm himself down, knowing he was going to really have to go to war with that family to keep them from turning me back over to the psychiatric facility where I'd spent the past nine years.

"I haven't heard from Trap since I sent the nigga the divorce papers. I know he got them because he returned the return of service receipt. I tried to send the nigga the motion I filed with the court for custody of Gia's kids. That shit came back undeliverable. The nigga is refusing mail at his address, *and* his mother fuckin' moved, so there's no telling where she is with your sister's kids," Rigel told me as I continued to paint.

"I have a plan to get those kids," I assured him.

"If you go anywhere near those kids while his mother has legal guardianship over those children, you'll be facing kidnapping charges, and they'll throw you right the fuck back in that fuckin' psych ward!" Rigel was angry with me. "Knight called my fuckin' office and told my assistant that I better bring Gia to him, or he was going to finish what his brother started. The nigga is threatening me to turn you back in and get Gia out of that facility. That's what he meant by that. He knows who the fuck you are, and unless I figure out a way to free you, too, both of you will never get out of that bitch! Do as I fuckin' say, Londyn!"

"Yes, Daddy..." I spoke softly.

The nigga was stunned, not quite sure how to respond to that. "Yo, don't do that. I'm fuckin' serious. The fact that you're still here and the police aren't at my door means he hasn't told Marley."

"He doesn't trust you *or* that bitch. She's the reason you knew exactly where to send the police that night Gia was arrested." I scoffed. "He feels she took my sister from him. He's angry at you, but she's who he's really upset with. I saw it in his face. Putting both me and Gia back in that place would make her happy, and that's the *last* thing that he wants. I think the nigga is gonna give you some time to figure out how to get her out, but once you do, I have a feeling that's when the nigga is gonna go to battle over her. I think a part of him was actually glad the woman here with his nephew isn't Gia. The nigga thinks he has a chance with her."

Rigel kicked his shoes off and walked over to the middle of the floor, where I sat on top of plastic, surrounded by buckets, bottles of paint, and damn canvas. "What you got going on, mama?" he asked.

I grinned up at him, "Art. Wanna color? Come on, take everything off. It's called body impression art."

"So, you want a nigga to sit my ass, dick, and balls on this shit?" Rigel looked at me like he wasn't about to dip his dick and balls in a bucket of paint.

"No, fool, I want you to let me rub the paint on you." I grabbed a tube of fire red acrylic paint.

Rigel still looked at me like I had the game messed up, but he started to undress anyway. "Can I ask you something?"

"Yeah." I watched him remove his crisp white shirt before walking over to drape it across one of the easels.

"Did you ever have kids?" he asked, walking back over to me while unzipping his pants.

I looked up at him, pursing my lips a little, not really feeling like discussing that shit. However, I was sure he had a valid reason for asking, so I answered. "No, but I wanted them. I can't have any. My ex-husband's brothers raped me with a metal pipe when I was twelve. To hush my foster parents up, the family paid my foster family off and agreed to continuously pay them if they married me to their oldest son. Been on the auction block all my life."

Rigel looked as though he hated that he even asked me the question in the first place. "Fuck. I'm sorry." He slipped out of his dark gray dress pants and kicked them over the floor. He stood before me in his fitted boxers, bulge staring me in the face.

I tried not to lick my lips as he pulled the boxers down, dick dropping out like an elephant trunk. "It's cool. It's over."

Rigel shook his head, watching me look back down at my artwork on the floor. "Do you know all these white muthafucka's addresses? Or do I have to look these niggas up?"

I laughed a little. "Yo, you already took out my sister's oppressor. Mine will get theirs in hell. It was the past. I don't have a future anyway."

"I'm working on getting you out of there so *I* can be your future. Or at least your present," Rigel confessed.

I don't know why my eyes instantly watered when he said that, but they did. I laughed a little to keep from crying. "Nigga, shut up."

I squirted paint into my hand and stood up from the plastic that I had spread out on the floor. Just as I stood, my dumb ass was about to slip and fall on my ass.

Rigel caught me by both wrists, pulling my painted body into his. To have a man who is strong enough to catch you when you fall is everything. It took everything in me right then not to ask that nigga to marry me. He stood me up straight, standing there with that perfectly carved chocolate body of his, looking down at me like he was waiting for me to put my hands on him.

"Not too much on my ass now. If I feel your fingers slip anywhere near my asshole, you're gonna wish you never picked up a paintbrush in your life," Rigel warned me as my hands touched his shoulders. "The shit is fuckin' cold, got damn. All this for art?"

"It's fun." I smiled a little at his body shivering under my touch. I spread the paint over his shoulders. "I haven't had a period since I was twelve," I told him, moving down to his chest. "It took until I was around you for my body to go back to normal. Thank you."

"I'm just glad to see you again." He looked my body over. "You look like Carrie with all this red paint." He chuckled a little as I smoothed the paint all over his chest and his abdomen. "Don't put that shit on my dick. Not trying to fuck up your pH."

I laughed out loud. "Oh, really? You just know I'ma give you some pussy?"

"I thought we were making body impression art? I'ma sit on this canvas, and you're gonna sit on top of me. Muthafuckas will know what type of impression we made when they see four hands and four feet on that bitch." He grinned down at me, biting his lip.

I looked up at him as he kissed my forehead. I sighed, rubbing the paint over his abdomen. It took everything in me not to reach around and grab those ass cheeks of his like he told me not to. I couldn't do anything but think of that man pressing my face into the canvas as he hit it hard from the back.

"I'm still trying to wrap my mind around the fact that I found you again." Rigel looked down at me, his eyes tracing my lips. "I think we should kiss."

I giggled like a schoolgirl as that man grabbed me by my neck, pulling my face to his so our lips could touch. I sighed heavily in that man's mouth as his lips stroked mine, and he nibbled on my lips a little. "You were gonna propose to my sister." I pulled my lips from his.

Rigel nodded. "I bought her a ring that costs the amount of a down payment for a house this size."

"Did you ever love her?" I asked, spreading paint over his chest and moving down his arms to his hands.

Rigel frowned. "I wanted to. I knew who she was when I

met her. I told you that. I knew I'd eventually run into you one way or another. I had to keep her close to bring you closer."

I frowned back, rubbing the paint onto both of his hands. "Your uncle says you used Marley to get to Gia."

Rigel's frown softened. "I guess the nigga does know me after all."

I shook my head at him. "That girl is in love with you."

Rigel disagreed. "She's in love with what she wishes her husband would do to her. She wants Knight to love her, not me. You need to worry about the nigga knowing that you're not Gia and not how his wife feels about a nigga she barely knows."

"*I* barely know you. You barely know me," I reminded him.

He didn't agree with that statement either. "You like art."

I nodded and squirted more paint into my hand before rubbing paint into his thighs. "I do. I kind of miss painting at the Bayou with the other psychopaths."

"You like nature." He looked into my face even though I was looking everywhere *but* his face. "I see the way you gaze out at the pond every morning. You're upset that your sister started chemotherapy, and you're not there with her."

I glanced up at his face. Brielle's page on Facebook was public. She hadn't posted anything, but one of her friends tagged her in a post of a picture of her sitting alongside her in chemo. Jaliyah had cervical cancer when we were just in middle school. She had to undergo chemotherapy after having a partial hysterectomy at such a young age.

"Nobody wants to be alone through chemo. So, no, I don't like it." I smacked my lips as he took the paint from my hands. I watched him squirt paint into his hands before handing the bottle back to me.

"You grew up wearing the most expensive clothes and shoes. Expensive perfume and jewelry, but I saw you ordering

Mixbar body spray from Target. All that money doesn't mean shit to you. You're a fuckin' millionaire, and you haven't spent more than a hundred dollars of that money. You could take that money and disappear, leaving your sister in that facility, but what you crave more than anything is attachment. You crave love, something you've never had." Rigel swore he was reading me.

And he was right, but I wasn't gonna let him think he was my new damn shrink. "I don't need a new therapist, Esquire."

"And," he spoke over me, "you like me."

I looked up at him, heart skipping beats. "I like *who*, nigga?"

"*Me,* muthafucka, you like me." Rigel liked playing games until people started to play back. Didn't take long for me to figure that out.

I shook my head, watching him walk over and sit on the damn canvas. He sat directly in the center of the canvas, exactly where I wanted him to sit. I turned around and walked over to him. I stood over him, gasping as he yanked me down, causing me to fall into his lap. I grinned a little, looking down at the canvas where our bodies made our initial prints. My knees straddled his waist. He leaned back, pressing both his hands into the black paint. And I leaned forward, pressing my hands into the paint just below his.

"You like me." Rigel looked into my face as I sighed at the feeling of his dick pressing against my pussy lips. He sat up. "Get up. Go over to that canvas over there and get on all fours, pressing your breasts against the paint. Arch that back as deep as you can get it."

I didn't hesitate to get up and walk over to the newly painted black canvas. I pressed my breasts against the paint, arching my back, ass in the air, as Rigel got up from the previous canvas that we were on. He walked over to me and got on his knees, smacking my right ass cheek, watching it jiggle.

"Is my bootyhole hairy? It's hard to shave that muthafucka." I looked back at him.

Rigel looked at my bootyhole, spreading my cheeks to get a closer look. "Nah, she looks smooth. You got all the hair," he said with all seriousness. He ran his fingers through my pussy lips before rubbing my bootyhole. "She's pretty."

"You gonna fuck me or what?" I asked, still looking back at him, watching him lick his lips at the sight of my insides.

"I don't know. Should I?" Rigel asked.

"All that shit you were just talkin' about putting my face down and my ass up. Don't fuckin' play with me," I demanded. "Beat this pussy like Ike. I don't care how much I run. You better pull me back and go deeper."

Rigel grinned mischievously like I didn't know what I'd just told him to do.

And no lie, I wasn't prepared for the way that man made love to me on that canvas. I felt like he flipped my cervix inside out on that floor. He had my pussy sounding like that beat on "The Percolator." I couldn't hold back the moans and screams no matter how hard I tried. He grasped my waist, pulling my body into his, throwing my ass back on his dick. And when I tried to run, he did as I asked and pulled me in deeper. The shit got so intense that my knees gave out after a few minutes, and I was flat on my stomach, arms stretched over my head, gripping the plastic laid out on the floor.

"*Mine.*" The nigga pressed his weight into my back. "Say that shit out loud so there's no confusion."

I shook my head, barely able to catch my breath, let alone say that foolish shit out loud.

He gripped my hair in his hands, growling in my ear. "Say this pussy is mine. Don't fuckin' play with me." He worked his pelvis, churning and digging into my soul like every inch of his dick was trying to feel every ripple inside me.

"Please, don't make me say that shit." I finally caught my breath. "You can't keep me."

"You got me fucked up if you think you're leaving me." Rigel lifted his body from mine a little. He bent my left leg, pushing it up and sliding it across the paint to get more access. He plundered my pussy until we came together, sighing and moaning in a quiet harmony.

He pulled out of me, and I peeled myself from the paint.

"We go together now," Rigel let me know as he paced his breathing to catch his breath.

I laughed and panted at the same time as I got up, looking at the mess we'd made on the canvas. "I'm definitely gonna call that painting "Fuckin'". I looked at him, black and red paint smeared all over him. "Oh, and what's this 'we go together now' shit? You speak French, Mr. Lawyer?"

Rigel frowned. "Nous sommes un couple," he said in French. "My mother's mother is from Cameroon. She taught me five languages, and you have me fucked up in all five, mama."

The doorbell rang.

Rigel looked at me before going over to the window to peep through the curtain. His eyebrows lowered, eyes squinting to get a closer view. "A burgundy Lexus just pulled up."

I gasped, rushing out of the room, careful not to slip on the floor. I hurried to the bathroom to grab my fuzzy bathrobe as the doorbell sounded again. I couldn't get to the front door fast enough. As soon as I opened the door, I fell into Jaliyah's arms.

"Bitch, you said Saturday!" I laughed and cried at the same time, pushing her off me.

"Girl, I was at the gas station a few minutes away when I told you that shit." She rolled her eyes, looking me over, eyeing the paint on my chest and hands. She looked down at the spots I'd just left on her blouse and pursed her lips. "You owe me another blouse. The fuck are you guys doing in here?" She looked over my shoulder.

I looked back to see Rigel strolling into the corridor in his flannel robe as well, looking like he'd just gone through a paintball war. I looked back at Jaliyah. "Art. Anyway, wait, how's Gia? Who's watching her if you're here?" I felt myself about to go into panic mode when Jaliyah grabbed my shoulders.

"Babe, Rigel didn't tell you?" Jaliyah asked as Rigel approached us.

I looked at Rigel and then back at her, lost. "Tell me what?"

"While they're investigating The Bayou, your sister has been moved to a state-owned facility. She's three and a half hours away in Wayne County. Rigel's investigation got her transferred to Cherry Hos—"

Jaliyah had barely gotten the information out when I started crying my eyes out, arms wrapped around Rigel.

"Yours," I answered him back from minutes earlier. "*All yours.*"

"That's what I thought." Rigel laughed, face buried in my neck, arms squeezing me back.

CHAPTER NINE
MARLEY

"Since Worth Law initiated an investigation on the Baltimore Bayou Psychiatric Facility, several allegations of rape, incest, and violent assaults have been reported," a news broadcaster on CNN announced on the morning of March 22nd. "The facility has been shut down, and all prisoners and patients have been transferred to state facilities throughout the country. The investigation was initiated when one of the inmates at the facility, celebrity wife, Gia Starr, alleged that her father, senatorial candidate Matthew Tiller, had been raping her while she was a patient at the hospital. Upon her release from the hospital, she claimed to have been brutally attacked by her father, who was attending a campaign event at a local hotel. Prestigious lawyer Rigel Worth, came to her aid, resulting in the death of Tiller and his security guards. One of the security guards verified the lawyer's story, only to die in the hospital of his wounds. Bob Sherriff is reporting from Cherry Hospital in Goldsboro with the latest news on a few of the transferred patients..."

"Why the fuck are you watching this shit?" Shiyah huffed,

sitting alongside me at the bar in Pink City, a sports bar/gentlemen's club in Uptown.

The girls thought they'd try taking me out to cheer me up, but it wasn't working. On almost every television at that bar, there was some reporter talking about that fuckin' medical facility that I'd visited a few weeks before it was shut down. I'd convinced Knight weeks ago to surveil that neighborhood in hopes of Gia showing up at Brielle's place. He'd yet to bring back news of whether he'd seen her, but a few days ago, he'd become much more distant than usual, which let me know he might have seen the bitch. She might've actually been Gia from the way he acted like his heart had shattered into pieces.

Knight had entirely shut down. With Gia out of the picture, I thought he'd try to make things work, but the exact opposite happened. It seemed that if he couldn't have us both, he didn't want either. Typical nigga shit. Wanted their fuckin' cake and to eat it to. But then again, I guess that's what you're supposed to do with fuckin' cake, right?

"I saw Brielle the other day at chemo." Spirit slid into the bar stool on the other side of me. "Homegirl looks depressed. Heard she's closing down her realty company for a little while. We're still keeping things afloat with SAFE, no thanks to Frankie." She rolled her eyes.

"Speaking of Frankie." Shiyah held her phone up to her face. "Look at this hoe."

We all looked over at Shiyah's iPhone 15 Pro Max display. Frankie was on the Napa wine train out in California, eating fancy food and shit in a pretty ass evening dress. She obviously wasn't alone because the person sitting across from her was filming. She was smiling and glowing.

"I've never seen her smile that hard," Shiyah commented.

"Hell yeah," Spirit chimed in, taking Shiyah's phone to get a closer look at the video. "The bitch done stole somebody's man." She watched Frankie toast with the person filming. She paused the video. "I wonder whose hand this is." Her eyes widened. "I'd know them tattoos on that nigga's hand anywhere! That's Trap Starr!" She pointed to the paused hand.

Shiyah and I looked at each other before laughing.

"The week that I've had, shit, I need that laugh." I sighed, laughing a little.

"Girl, you remember when I paid $4789.54 cents for the ultimate VIP package last year to see Trapp on tour? This is that nigga's hand!" Spirit told us over our laughter.

"That nigga is on tour." Shiyah rolled her eyes, signaling the bartender to come over so she could have her third lemon drop. She pointed to all three of our empty glasses. "Three more," she mouthed when the bartender made it halfway across the bar toward us before nodding and turning around to get to our drink order. Shiyah looked back at Spirit, who was searching through her IG feed to find Trapp's tour schedule.

"See!" Spirit's eyes lit up. "The nigga was in Inglewood yesterday. He's probably still *in* California! It's only seven hours from Napa County. And have y'all *seen* Frankie in the past few weeks? She's got her cousins running her office. You over here worried about the news, and Frankie is out there getting payback. I'm tellin' you, Frankie is hunchin' on Gia's husband. Ouuuu, y'all bitches are messy. I'm tellin' you, if I catch any of you hoes on my nigga, I'm gonna get to slicing. I'll go to hell or jail about my nigga."

"Which nigga?" Shiyah and I muttered at the same time.

"All of them!" Spirit snapped. "Don't touch nann one of them. Shit. I'm just saying. That nigga she's with is Trapp. I heard her cousins talking today at the real estate office. They said Frankie put in an appeal for that child support case."

"Hell yeah. It came into my office today." Rigel's voice resonated through my eardrums.

I looked over to see Rigel across the bar, signaling me to come over. That nigga had some nerve, but I found myself getting up from my seat.

"Girl, you better not!" Shiyah squealed, trying to grab my arm.

I pulled away from her, waving her off. "Bitch, I'm just going to talk to the man. Nothing major, damn."

I could smell that man's cologne before I was even a few feet from him. I had to talk my hormones down as I sat two stools away from him. The bartender set my drink in front of me before going over to give my two nosey friends their drinks.

"The fuck are you doing here?" I asked Rigel.

Rigel looked at me, trying to gauge my frame of mine before he spoke. "Tell your brother-in-law his baby's mama is fighting back. She has new representation who may help her get those kids back. I'm no longer his attorney, so I'll be returning the motion to the sender. Just thought you should prepare Pops."

Shadow was going crazy at his place with those kids. Trying to nurse Brielle through her chemo and postpartum depression was hard enough, then two bad ass kids on top of that. He was going through it. And Rigel was definitely enjoying the fact that he was about to go through more.

"Misery sure does love fuckin' company." I rolled my eyes.

"Who's miserable?" Rigel made a face. "I'm happy."

"Are you?" I asked. "It's gotta suck being in love when the law doesn't agree."

Rigel just looked at me, that same look he'd give when he was trying to figure out how much a person really knew. He was too smart to fall for just anything a person threw at him. I was used to playing mind games and tossing out leading questions. That, we had in common.

"You think me and Gia are in love?" Rigel scoffed.

"No. I don't think you're in love with Gia at all," I stated, hoping he'd give some sort of indication of whether or not that girl at his place was really Gia's sister.

"Trap wanted me to keep her away from Knight, and that's what I'm doing, ma. That's it. Minding my business isn't gonna do shit but get your heart broken." Rigel picked up his shot glass and tossed it back. "And tell ya nigga if he comes looking for trouble again, it's gonna come find him. Gia is not his problem, so he doesn't need to make her his problem."

"I hear the prisoners and patients were transferred to other facilities when The Baltimore Bayou was closed down." I continued to pry.

Rigel laughed out loud. "Ma, you *really* wanna go this route? What happened to these twins is about to be that woman's get out of jail free card. I'm reopening the twin's case."

"What is she in for? How did Gia's twin end up at the same mental institution in the first place?" I asked.

The light in Rigel's eyes dimmed. "Like I said, don't go looking for trouble, or it will come find you. Leave it alone. Just tell your brother-in-law he's about to lose two more sons."

I went home that night to find Knight sitting outside on the porch steps, a bottle of Henny in his hands. It must've been around 11:00. He was usually out somewhere with his brother or homeboys, but he was just sitting there, looking like he wasn't sure what to do about life.

I walked over and sat beside him, my eyes tracing his handsome profile.

"They moved Gia's sister to Cherry Hospital out in Wayne County," he told me without even looking me in the face.

I hesitated. "Hello to you too, boo."

Knight looked at me before looking back out into the night sky. "Her sister's name is Londyn Lepont. She was committed to the Bayou after killing her mother-in-law. Londyn's foster family owns the Bayou. She'll probably end up getting out of that facility after all this shit comes out about how she ended up with that Lepont family in the first place. There's more to her story; there always is. Are you satisfied now?"

"Why would I be satisfied?" I resented that.

"You put Gia back in that fuckin' hell hole because of me," Knight told me, watching me shake my head. "Nah, you put her in that muthafucka to hurt me. And you were fuckin' Rigel. How long had you been fuckin' him? Was it before you found the fuckin' earring? Was it before you knew about us?"

I turned to him. "Gia came here, having everyone believe that Trap was beating her when that shit was all in her head! She came into my fuckin' office, making jokes about my mother's pastor raping me! And you didn't even come home the night I made those blueberry pancake biscuits! I—"

"I asked you a fuckin' question." Knight's voice grew louder.

"I knew the night you came home only to shower, then went to work early, that you fucked that bitch," I snapped. "You hadn't touched me in months before Gia popped up, but you couldn't look me in the face for a week after I made those fuckin' biscuits. I knew then that I had lost you. That night I went to Ashville is the night another man showed me the attention that you've *never* shown me!"

"And it kills you right now that he's showing that same attention to the same woman who I was fuckin', doesn't it?" Knight laughed a little before sipping from his bottle.

I looked at him. I wanted to get mad, but I couldn't. I knew right then that the woman living with Rigel couldn't be Gia.

Knight wouldn't have been laughing at another man fuckin' the love of his life, but he'd damn sure laughed at me for thinking I was the only bitch some random nigga was fuckin'. If the woman with Rigel was definitely Gia, Knight wouldn't wait for Shadow to tell him when to make a move. Knight didn't give a fuck that Rigel was his nephew. All he would give a fuck about was that Gia was fuckin' another nigga. He went out of his way to find out the name of the other twin and where she was located so he'd know where to find Gia. He'd found out the twins switched places, but he wasn't going to tell me until he had to.

"Well, Rigel's working on gathering information to get Londyn out of that place. Why he cares so much about either of them, I'm not sure." I exhaled deeply, grabbing the bottle of Henny from him and taking a few sips.

"Londyn and Rigel went to the same private school for a while in Maryland when Agnes was hiding from Shadow," Knight told me. "That's probably when they met. Childhood friends, or at least knew of each other."

I looked at him. "How do you know this?"

"Shadow's been looking up information on Rigel all month, trying to figure out where Rigel's been. The nigga's been feeling guilty instead of angry at what the nigga's family has done to our family. Rigel is a beast in the courtroom; I'll give him that. I'm sure he'll find a way to get Londyn out of that facility and reunite with her sisters. That's why I'm leaving him alone for now. The nigga is helping these twins to fuck with us. I'm sure one or both of them will talk Brielle into leaving Shadow, or better yet, Rigel will do something to bring down our medical system. I don't put shit past the nigga, but he has a plan. His mother has a fuckin' plan, and you hired her as one of our midwives?" Knight growled at me.

"I hired her before I knew the family's fucked up history!" I exclaimed. "I hired her to piss you off because she's Rigel's mother!"

Knight shook his head. "As of today, you have no more hiring or firing power. That bitch made a tea that could've cost Brielle her fuckin' life!"

"A tea that has been in her family for generations to assist women with expelling dead babies." I huffed. "It eliminates the D&C process."

"It can cause a pregnant woman to hemorrhage!" Knight howled. "Shadow was going to kill Rigel and his mother that fuckin' night! The only thing that stopped him was his two-year-old having an asthma attack that night. That was the night he found out that the baby had been dead for days before Brielle was drugged. Brielle had to find out she had a fuckin' tumor, that her baby was dead, and that she would never be able to have fuckin' kids like that. The nigga is at his office right now instead of out there at his lakehouse. He's got a nanny and a nurse back in Lexington with Brielle. You caused all this fuckin' drama by trying to hurt a nigga who you knew from jump was in love with someone else! You can't keep blaming me when you knew how I felt about her!"

"A lot of people never get over their first love, Knight," I told myself for probably the thousandth time. "She was your first, and I was hoping I'd be your last love. I didn't realize until I saw her again that she'd broken a heart that I could never heal. The moment I saw her at your sister's house, I knew my world was over. It took her days to tear down what I built with you in eleven years! She shook your world when she left you at that group home! I saw your face the day she got married! I gave you two beautiful children, but nothing I could give you could replace the life you wanted with her. You are broken, and I broke myself trying to fuckin' fix you!"

Knight's face remained emotionless as he chugged the bottle down until it was damn near half-full.

I laughed a little. "You just want me here to catch you when you fall, but who's gonna catch me while I'm fuckin' patching you up and mending your fuckin' wounds?" I got up from the porch and walked toward my car.

"The fuck are you going?" Knight leaned back on the porch, probably too drunk to even come after me.

"Like you give a fuck," I snapped, getting into my car.

Just as Knight said, Shadow was in his office, working off the clock like he'd told us not to do on several occasions.

I tapped at his door. "I thought you said no doing company work when we're not on company time?" I rolled my eyes a little, my trench coat draped over my arm as I walked into the office.

Shadow removed his glasses from his face, eyeing me in my A-line spaghetti-strap dress. "Classy dress to wear to the club with those ratchet nurses you like to kick it with. They came in here drunk a little while ago, and they're sleeping upstairs in the doctor's headquarters. They're supposed to be at work for third shift, which *they* both volunteered for, yet them bitches are hungover. They better be up in an hour, or they're fuckin' fired. I'm not hiring any more of your friends."

"My friends keep this muthafucka afloat and your patients entertained." I rolled my eyes, walking over to sit in the chair in front of his desk. "You have patients who ask for Shiyah, Spirit, and Jasmine specifically like they're strippers or some shit. Ginger applied last week. I told you that you need to hire her to show that your company is diverse. I also hired a few midwives."

Shadow looked at me while leaning back in his swivel chair. "Knight told me that you hired Agnes. You're trying to get your sneaky link's mama killed, huh? Her family has pull, but so do I. I could kill her without getting my hands dirty. When I was just a teenager, her father showed me how to mix this chemical that could melt bones. I can get rid of someone without leaving a trace, thanks to that family. There will be no body to bury. Nothing left of her to prove she even existed."

"Except for her son," I reminded him. "*Your* son."

Shadow grabbed his water bottle and guzzled it down. I knew Patron when I smelled that shit. He and his brother drank their problems away. I wasn't one to talk. I'd had one too many lemon drops and damn sure shouldn't have been driving. Thank God for Driver's Assist, or my car definitely wouldn't have stayed within the lines to get to Shadow that night.

"The fuck do you want, Marley?" Shadow set the bottle down on the desk.

"I saw Rigel at the lounge today. He said Frankie's new lawyer sent him a motion for appeal on that child custody case." I watched Shadow look unbothered. "You're gonna need a lawyer because Rigel's not your lawyer, obviously."

"I didn't fire the nigga." Shadow laughed a little.

I shook my head. "You can't be fuckin' serious. You seriously expect him to defend your case after all that's happened?"

"Shit, he started this game when he defended me in court, knowing I didn't remember who he was. He had a solid case against Frankie, helped me get my kids, and he's gonna help me keep them. It's alright. I'll be at the law firm on Monday," Shadow assured me.

"That nigga hates you for whatever you did to him. Just leave him alone before shit gets any worse." I draped my jacket across the back of the chair. "That boy is coming for whatever he feels you took from him. I know a revenge plot when I see it. He's technically a Shade. He's probably entitled to the profits of this hospital or maybe your family's inheritance. Did you specifically list your children on that will? Who did you list as your beneficiaries in case something should happen to you? Your sister? Knight? Stratus and Cloudy?"

"You." Shadow laughed to himself.

I was confused. "Me?"

"If something happened to me, Sable wouldn't know the first thing about running this place." Shadow shook his head. "Knight lives by emotions. As soon as he smells scrambled eggs, toast, and pancakes in the morning, he comes in this muthafucka, telling half the staff they can take paid leave if they want. Stratus and Cloudy can't touch anything I leave for them until they are eighteen because you know Frankie will spend their money on bundles and lashes.

"I thought you gave a fuck about your bro until I found out your hired Agnes. Brielle is my fuckin' everything, and that bitch could've killed her. Rigel knew what his mother did and was trying to hurt Brielle to hurt me for hurting him. Brielle won't even let me hold her or touch her. She wouldn't even let me go with her to chemo. She's depressed and lonely. Shit, *I'm* depressed and lonely. She wants a relationship, something I don't even know anything about. The last relationship I had was with Agnes, and look how the fuck that turned out."

"Healing takes time." I crossed my legs. "And sometimes time doesn't even help. But running sure as fuck doesn't help. If you love Brielle, you'll support her through her pain. She just lost your child and can't have any more. Did you have a funeral for the baby? Did you even *see* the baby?"

Shadow exhaled deeply. "Brielle asked that Justice be cremated. She didn't want a funeral. She didn't want to see or hold the baby after they removed her, but I saw her when they removed Brielle's uterus and cut her out of it. I'll never get the chance to have another child, Marley."

I looked at him. "Because Brielle won't be able to give you a baby? See, that means you *do* want a relationship with her, after all. Quit acting like you don't love that girl, bro."

Shadow shook his head, putting his glasses back on. "I have paperwork. I don't have time to bullshit with you."

"Your brother told me today that Rigel is working on trying to get Gia's twin, Londyn, out. Rigel's a great lawyer; he's won some very big cases. The Tillers are probably waiting for him to make the wrong move so they can take him out for what happened to Gia's father. Digging up dirt on Londyn's family will bring more harm his way, and I really don't think Gia is Gia. I think they found a way to switch places. I think Gia is sitting in that psychiatric hospital, and the woman at Rigel's place is really Londyn! Why else hasn't Knight gone after her?" I exclaimed.

Shadow looked at me like he was sick of hearing about me and my problems. "Man, let it go. You could've cost us a fuckin' lawsuit. You knew Brielle's baby was dead, and you didn't tell her. Then, you hire my baby mama. What are you trying to do? Destroy us? Fuck up your career? You're gonna ruin your own life trying to fuck up not just your life but the rest of ours. I didn't want to find out like this that Rigel is my son."

"And I'm sorry about that," I tried to tell him.

Shadow's temples twitched. "No, you're not. You want everyone to hurt just like you're hurting. Knight is my baby brother, and I love him, but you need to realize that he doesn't love you. You gave your all, but it'll never be enough for a man who's in love with another woman. He forgot about you. Remember that shit and move the fuck on."

I laughed at his advice. "So, you're a fuckin' expert now?"

Shadow disagreed. "Nah, but I've fucked up enough to know when it's time to let go." Shadow's phone chimed on his desk. His cell phone was right in front of me. It chimed again.

That time, it said some bitch's name that wasn't Brielle's, and it said *sent attachment*.

I grabbed the phone. He and Knight were the only niggas I knew who didn't have a screen lock on their phones. Shadow always said if a bitch wanted to look at his phone and cry herself to sleep at night, that was on her. Whoever the bitch was, Shadow didn't want me to see because his ass couldn't get up from the chair fast enough.

I swiped up to see who'd sent the message. My eyes widened when I saw that Jaliyah Marcus, that doctor from The Bayou was sending Shadow attachments. I barely opened the message to see the bitch naked, wearing nothing but heels and a damn stethoscope.

Shadow tried to grab the phone from me, but I hid the phone behind my back. "Stop fuckin' playing with me."

"Nigga, you're fuckin' Dr. Marcus?" I laughed in disbelief. "So *that's* how Knight knows about Londyn? How long have you been fuckin' her?"

"That's *Knight's* phone." Shadow watched the smile wipe clean from my face. "Bro left his phone here a few hours ago."

"Oh, my goodness." I got up from the chair, feeling sick to my stomach. "The nigga is fuckin' her doctor to get information about her? I need to get out of here!"

"Sis, you're drunk. You shouldn't have even driven here." Shadow grabbed my arm before I could stumble out of his office door. "Come here, don't cry."

It was too late. I was already crying.

He walked me over to his sofa to sit down. He sat down beside me and wrapped me in his arms as I cried on his shoulder. "Just let him go, babe. He'll do whatever to get that girl back. It's time to take your kids and walk out the door."

"Nobody wants to be alone!" I cried.

"You're already alone," Shadow reminded me. "Being alone

when you're in a relationship is the worst place to be. If you need a place to stay for a few days, you and the boys can crash at my place. I'm over in Lexington with Bri'. Y'all can stay there for as long as you need to."

"So your bitches can jump me in my sleep?" I lifted my head from his shoulders, drying my face. "Nah, I'm good. I'll figure this out on my own."

Shadow pushed my locs from my face and gently kissed my forehead the way Rigel once had. I looked up at him as he kissed my nose that time. And I gasped as he gently kissed my lips.

And I kissed the nigga back. We both kind of looked at each other like we couldn't believe we'd just kissed.

"We've been drinking." I sighed heavily.

Shadow agreed. "Yeah, but shit felt good, didn't it?"

"But I'm married to your brother." I attempted to get up from the chair. I wasn't too drunk to realize what I wanted to do was wrong, no matter how good it felt.

"So?" Shadow pulled me back down.

"There would be no coming back from this," I told him to his face, that handsome face.

"Coming back to what? A husband who'd fuck his side chick's doctor for information?" Shadow laughed, getting up from the sofa. "Yeah, okay. We're drunk. You don't need to drive. Go upstairs and go to sleep on one of the bunks." He went back over to his leather swivel chair and went back to work.

I got up from the sofa, thinking as I walked toward the door.

"Don't forget your coat," Shadow reminded me. "And lock my door on your way out."

I sighed, locking the office door and stepping out of my

heels. I turned around, unbuttoned my dress, and walked back over to Shadow.

Shadow scooted his chair back from his desk as I walked up to him, stepping out of my dress. He pulled my body closer to his, and I slid onto his lap, legs straddling his hips as he grabbed me in for a kiss.

I'd lost his brother. Shit, his son used me. Why not? Right?

ALSO BY KRYSTAL ARMSTEAD

Saved By The Millionaire Next Door

I Let A Country Boy Get Me Pregnant 3

I Let A Country Boy Get Me Pregnant 2

I Let A Country Boy Get Me Pregnant

A Single Woman & The Thug Next Door 3

A Single Woman & The Thug Next Door 2

A Single Woman & The Thug Next Door

When They See Us Together 2

When They See Us Together

On Every Thug I Love

Printed in the USA
CPSIA information can be obtained
at www.ICGtesting.com
LVHW041144230524
781080LV00001B/53